SECRET NINJA SPIES

Josh scanned the room. Two big men in black. Three slick Yakuza. And there was a commotion from the stairs as the two Chinese bouncers burst into the room, flexing their muscles.

Seven against two. I've seen better odds...

Granny and Yoshida spun into the room, ducking and parrying each other's blows.

Eight against three. Not much better... *Granny hit one of the men in black in the back of the neck, and he crumpled at once.* Except one of our three is Granny!

SECRET NINJA SPIES

FOOTBALL FRENZY

ALEX KO

USBORNE

With special thanks to Rosie Best
For Mum, Dad and Lizzie

First published in the UK in 2011 by Usborne Publishing Ltd., Usborne House,
83-85 Saffron Hill, London EC1N 8RT, England. www.usborne.com

Series created by Working Partners Limited.
Text copyright © Working Partners Limited, 2011
Illustrations copyright © Usborne Publishing Ltd., 2011
Illustrations by Kanako and Yuzuru.

The name Usborne and the devices ♀ ⊕ are Trade Marks of
Usborne Publishing Ltd.

A CIP catalogue record for this book is available from the British Library.

ISBN 9781409521976

Chapter One

Josh Murata ducked to avoid another punch. *I'm done for*, he thought.

The black-clad figure in front of him twisted, one foot slicing towards Josh's legs. Josh threw himself into a backflip and, for a moment, the world tipped upside down. He landed perfectly – and just in time to see his opponent's other foot soaring towards his nose. He fell back onto his hands as the kick scythed through the empty air where his head had just been.

Then, springing back up, Josh launched a spinning heel kick, giving a triumphant shout of *"Hai!"* But the fighter's arms were a blur and, suddenly, Josh's foot was trapped in the grip of his opponent's hands! The next thing he knew, he'd been lifted off the floor and was spinning through the air. He just had time to tuck his arms in and roll as he hit the tatami mat.

How can I defeat such a master? Josh thought, scrambling to his feet. *I haven't landed a single blow!* He gasped in a few breaths and planted himself in a fighting stance, ready for his opponent's next move.

But the figure had turned its back, as if the fight was over. Josh readied himself, his heart racing – now was his chance...

He hesitated.

Should I strike my opponent in the back?

The fighter turned a stern, wrinkled face to look at him. Her grey eyes glinted. "You hesitate to strike me?" she asked.

"Well...yes, Granny," Josh said.

"Never hesitate." Granny Murata gave him a severe look. "Do not think of this as merely training in the dojo – you must treat each lesson as though it's a

fight to the death. The ninja is not without honour, but he or she must be practical in all things."

Josh bowed. "Yes, *obaasan*."

Granny returned the bow, then straightened her black ninja training outfit. Josh was sweating right through his white martial arts uniform, but she didn't have a single silver hair out of place. She might have been demonstrating the slow, graceful movements of the tea ceremony instead of how to defeat an opponent in close combat.

They crossed the huge dojo, walking along polished wooden paths between large squares of tatami matting. On some of the mats, fighters dressed in black or white were sparring, using smooth wrestling moves, high-tech riot gear or gleaming silver swords.

Josh still couldn't quite believe that this place was hidden underneath a central Tokyo park, around the back of his granny's retirement home. And what's more, the dojo was only a small part of the top-secret government facility!

His twin sister Jessica was stretching out her muscles at the edge of the dojo, below a large painting of a tiger stalking through the undergrowth.

Josh's heart gave a twist as he saw the painting. It reminded him of his parents, who were far away in Africa, travelling as emergency surgeons with *Médecins sans Frontières*. They emailed whenever they could, but internet access was a luxury. He missed them, but felt proud that they were out there, battling against war and disease. When they'd extended their trip, Josh and Jessica had been only too happy to stay with their granny for a few more weeks.

And why wouldn't they? The twins were already having an unbelievable time in Japan. On their very first day, a mysterious, black-clad figure had rescued them from an attacker on the streets of Tokyo. They'd unmasked the figure, and discovered it was none other than their own 65-year-old granny! Once the secret was out, Granny ended up telling them all sorts of things even their parents didn't know about; like the hidden buttons and passages that led from Granny's apartment to the entrance of Team O's underground headquarters. Team Obaasan, to give it its full title, was a group of crack crime-fighters who all turned out to be... geriatrics! And Granny, it seemed, was their leader.

After that, Granny had had a hard time keeping

them away from the action. The twins were soon embroiled in a mission to rescue a Japanese pop star from the clutches of the Yakuza, a ruthless gang of organized criminals led by 78-year-old Yoshida Noburu, an old enemy of Granny's. It had all worked out well in the end, though – and now they couldn't wait to put their new and improved ninja skills into action again!

Jessica and Josh both bowed to Granny and then walked back to the changing rooms together to swap their white training uniforms for their normal clothes.

"Nice one," Jessica grinned. "That was a great backflip. You've really got the hang of safe falling, too. I thought you were going to end up with concussion at *least*."

"Yeah," Josh replied, rubbing the side of his cheek. He could still feel the ridged pattern of the tatami mats printed on his skin. "Thanks. You did pretty well against her too. That scissor kick was awesome. I think we lost less badly today than yesterday, right?"

"Oh yeah," Jessica laughed. "We're definitely losing less badly every day. And just think, if someone had told you a few weeks ago that you'd be really happy to be fighting your granny and only getting pummelled a *little* bit..."

"I would've told them they were mad," Josh said.

"I'm having a pretty good summer, how about you?" Jessica asked.

"Best summer ever," Josh agreed.

The polished metal elevator doors slid open with a beep and a swish, to reveal the gleaming headquarters of Team Obaasan.

Josh and Jessica exchanged grins. When they'd first been introduced to Granny Murata's secret team of elderly ninjas, this place had taken Josh's breath away with its banks of monitors, the control panel covered in hundreds of buttons and dials, the wall of polished weapons, and the high-tech grappling hooks and harnesses that hung from an old-fashioned hatstand in one corner.

But as Josh looked around now, it felt kind of like home, even though the scene could easily have belonged to a mad sci-fi anime film.

Granny nodded at two people standing beside the racks of weaponry. "Sachiko-san, Mimasu-san," she said, using the polite, proper Japanese address.

Josh's eyebrows twitched. He recognized Sachiko, the Team O mistress of disguises, smiling at the twins with a pair of sparkling dentures. But the other one looked nothing like Mimasu, the team's elderly, female technology expert. This was a middle-aged man. How could Granny have mistaken him for Mimasu?

Sachiko adjusted the man's collar and smoothed down his sideburns, then frowned. She folded her arms and her collection of faded tattoos wrinkled up around her elbows.

"Hmm. This prosthetic isn't sticking right. Let me put a little more glue around the edge."

She bent over a little table covered in pots and tubes and brushes. The man turned to smile at the twins, and Josh gasped. It *was* Mimasu! He could just about recognize the glint in her eye, but the rest of her face was totally different.

Sachiko winked at the twins as she straightened up, holding a pot of glue and a tiny spatula. "Do you like my latest masterpiece?" she asked. "Mimasu-san, give us a twirl and let the kids see what a little latex and paint can do."

Josh and Jessica approached as Mimasu turned

slowly on the spot. Josh could hardly believe it was her. She was still the tallest of Team O, but she'd lost at least twenty-five years and gained a jutting chin and a moustache.

"Mostly prosthetics," Sachiko explained. Josh cringed as she appeared to dig a scalpel into part of Mimasu's skin, underneath one of the sideburns, but when he looked closer he saw that it was just latex, painted to match the flesh around it perfectly. "I wish I could sell my de-aging technique in Hollywood," she added, a little wistfully. "Unfortunately, it's a Japanese state secret."

"I should be going," Mimasu said. It was a shock to hear her old lady's voice coming from the lips of a younger man. "I need to be at the embassy before two o'clock."

"A mission?" Jessica asked Granny. Granny pursed her lips in an "It's confidential" way. "Oh…right. *Top secret.* I guess we're not needed on this one."

Not needed? No way! Josh was determined to find out how he and his twin could help. What else were they going to do? Another day's training at the dojo sounded so tame when they could be getting involved in some real ninja action.

Mimasu and Sachiko walked out through the heavy metal door that led to Team O's workshops, passing Mr. Yamamoto on his way in. The tanned old weapons expert grinned and waved to Josh. "Hi there," he said. "How was your training today?"

"It was great—" Josh began. Granny coughed pointedly. "Er – I mean – *jisshuu yokatta...desu?*"

"Very good." Mr. Yamamoto smiled, the skin on his face wrinkling up like a raisin. "And your Japanese is improving as well! So, what do you have planned for the rest of your stay in Tokyo? When you're not helping us fight crime, that is."

Josh grinned. "Football! We're going to the big match tomorrow."

"Japan versus Portugal," Jessica added, excitedly. "It's going to be *awesome*. Apparently all the tickets have sold out!"

Mr. Yamamoto raised an eyebrow. "How did you manage to get hold of some?" he asked.

"You remember Kiki?" Jessica said. Kiki was the pop star Team O had rescued from the Yakuza – she and the twins had become good friends.

"Indeed," said Mr. Yamamoto. "Who could forget such a stunning young lady?"

"Yamamoto-san," Granny snapped. "Please act your age."

Mr. Yamamoto winked at Josh.

Josh remembered Mr. Yamamoto's tales of his various wives and tried not to snigger. "Anyway," he said, "Kiki is friends with Shinichiro Hanzo – he's the best goalkeeper in the J League, maybe in the *world* – and she got us tickets to watch the match and I..." Josh finally had to pause for breath. "...can't wait."

"If he's as good as you say, I should put some money on Japan winning their match against England this Saturday!" Mr. Yamamoto said.

"Gambling is a filthy habit," said Granny sternly.

"Well...if everybody's putting bets on Japan, the odds won't be very good anyway." Mr. Yamamoto smiled. "Have fun at the game, you two – it'll be more exciting than hanging around with us old people, eh?"

"Yeah, right!" Josh said, as he watched Mr. Yamamoto pick up a pair of long, gleaming katanas from the weapons rack and head for the Team O combat practice room.

"Now," said Granny, "wait here while I fetch my equipment, then we can return to the apartment and I shall make you a nice healthy lunch."

She left through another of the heavy doors.

"Nice healthy lunch…" Jessica repeated after their granny had gone. "I can't wait."

"Yeah, tofu…" Josh deadpanned. "It's my favourite, right after salad."

Jessica gave him a lopsided grin. This was "old normal" Granny for you – the way she had always been before they'd discovered her secret. But now they knew about her other side, they could forgive her the healthy-eating obsession.

Granny walked back in and Josh glanced around the headquarters again while they waited for the elevator. Excitement was building in his chest, and it wasn't just about the football. Life with "secret ninja" Granny was so much more interesting than before. You never knew what to expect next. Any day now they could be off on another mission, fighting crime and saving Tokyo. He had to make it happen. *It's what we were meant to do*, he thought, drawing in a deep breath. *I'm ready!*

Chapter Two

The crowd filled the Ajinomoto Stadium with waves of noise that echoed between the huge screens advertising fizzy drinks. One of the screens flashed up the score: *EXTRA TIME: JAPAN 1 – PORTUGAL 0.*

It was hot and humid, and even though it was a Tuesday afternoon, the stadium was crammed to the roof with supporters from both teams. Josh leaned forward, his heart in his mouth, as out on the pitch a Portuguese striker turned on his heel and managed to get the ball past the Japanese defenders.

"No!" Kiki squealed, hunched down in the seat next to Josh, half-hiding behind her Japan scarf. The striker barrelled towards the goal with the defenders in his wake. Josh could feel the crowd around him breathing in, clutching their flags, all eyes on the white figure in goal.

"Save it, Shini..." Josh muttered.

The striker feinted right, then sent the ball arcing towards the left side of the goal. Shini leaped like a cat, snatching the ball just before it crossed the goal line. He landed and rolled, the ball safely cradled to his chest.

The crowd went crazy, leaping out of their seats and roaring, as he stood up and booted the ball down the pitch to the waiting feet of a Japanese midfielder. He turned to the home fans and raised both hands in triumph.

"Go Shini! *Hai, hai, hai!*" Kiki shrieked happily, leaping out of her seat. Josh could hear the triumph in the singing of the Japanese fans, even though he couldn't catch any of the words.

"It's not quite over yet..." Jessica said. She was

glancing from the action to her watch, to her reporter's pad full of scrawled notes and back to the pitch, her face full of tension. "Come on, ref, blow the whistle!"

The Portuguese and Japanese players were scrapping over the ball in the centre circle, fighting for control...

Then the huge speakers hanging over the crowd relayed the piercing shriek of a whistle, and down on the pitch, the referee held up his hand.

The crowd roared again. Kiki screamed for joy, the strength of her popstar lungs making Josh's ears ache.

"Come on!" she said, flinging her scarf over her shoulder. "Let's go down and congratulate him."

"Congratulate who?" asked Jessica.

"Shini, of course!"

The twins shared a glance. "Erm...okay!"

Josh tried to look cool and casual – but it was hard when he was being waved through a VIP door and into the backstage corridors of an international stadium. The place was massive. It probably wasn't any bigger than the football stadiums back home, but these bare, harshly-lit corridors felt like an endless labyrinth. Finally, they came to a lift, which took them down to *another* corridor.

As they walked, Jessica put a hand over her nose. "What's that smell?"

Josh grimaced. "I think it's...*feet*."

"This is more like the PE changing room at school than an international stadium," Jessica sniffed.

"I suppose feet smell the same pretty much anywhere..." Josh said.

"Ah, here," said Kiki. "Locker rooms." She pushed open a swinging door, and the twins followed her through into a large area full of wide wooden benches, lockers, and walls lined with hooks. The room was empty. Josh felt his heart sink. Had Shini already left?

"We did take a while to get here," Kiki said, "I guess they've all changed. Maybe he's waiting upstairs..."

"Wait," said Jessica. "Did you hear that?" She walked over to an archway in the wall. An identical room lay on the other side, and as Josh walked up behind her he heard it too – *voices*.

"*No*," one of them said. "No. I will not."

Josh peered round the archway, and saw a man

standing between two rows of wooden benches. It was him. Shini. He'd obviously showered and changed – his hair was wet and he was wearing clean tracksuit bottoms and a blue Team Japan jacket. Josh couldn't believe he was so close to a genuine football legend... but there was something wrong. Shini didn't look happy. His arms were folded and his shoulders hunched, and he was glaring at a man wearing a large overcoat, a hat and a scarf wrapped high around his neck. *That's odd,* thought Josh. *What's he doing bundled up like that in this heat?*

Shini looked up and saw Kiki and the twins. The other man moved, raising his head as if glancing at them too, but the hat and scarf meant that Josh couldn't see his face. Then he strode off through a door, slamming it behind him.

"Hey, Shini," Kiki said softly, stepping into the room. "Are you all right? What was all that about?"

"Oh...nothing," Shini said, shrugging. He looked uncomfortable, but then he gave Kiki a welcoming smile. "He was just a fan. A bit...intense. They ask you very odd things sometimes. But you know all about that."

"I do," Kiki laughed, and it seemed to brighten Shini's mood. He grinned at her, then at Josh and Jessica. Josh beamed back.

"That was amazing!" he blurted out. "The match, I mean. You were great."

"*Dōmō arigatō*," said Shini. "Thank you."

"Shini," Kiki said, "these are my friends, Josh and Jessica Murata. They're half English, visiting from London."

"Oh really?" said Shini, still smiling. "Who will you be cheering for at the weekend? England or Japan?"

Josh threw a glance at his sister. "Er...well, England's our team really," he admitted.

"But you know, we're half Japanese too, so I think... the best team should win," Jessica said.

Shini laughed. "Good answer! England will be tough. Neil Ash's right foot is my personal worst enemy this week."

"But England's weaker in defence now that Nick Johnson's got a leg injury," Josh pointed out.

Kiki's head dropped, and she made a loud snoring sound. Everyone laughed. "Sorry, Kiki," Shini said, patting her shoulder. His hand lingered there and she flashed him a smile, her cheeks colouring.

Even Josh could smell romance in the air. Jessica was staring straight at Kiki and Shini.

"Soooo," she said. "Is there something you two want to tell us? Are you guys maybe...*more* than just friends?"

Kiki blushed a little more and looked at Shini, who shrugged and nodded. "It's a big secret," she said. "You have to promise not to put it in any of your articles for the school paper – the tabloids would go crazy for this news! The paparazzi already follow us wherever we go, but we don't want to give them confirmation just yet."

"But how did you first meet?" Jessica asked. "When did you first clap eyes on each other?"

"Shini came to the first *Banzai Banzai Benzaiten* show," said Kiki. "We met afterwards and, well..."

"Let us just say...we have seen a lot of each other since then," Shini said.

Josh smiled at them, and at the ecstatic look on Jessica's face. He knew what she was thinking: if it hadn't been for Team O, Kiki would never have made it to the first episode of *Banzai Banzai Benzaiten*, her new live music show. It was as if they'd brought Kiki and Shini together!

"In fact," said Shini, "Kiki's coming to dinner at my parents' restaurant tonight. You should join us."

"Oh," Josh said, heart sinking. "We would love to. But we're staying with our granny, and I think she's taking us out to eat tonight."

"Bring her to Shini's place!" Kiki clapped her hands together. "Dinner's on me – after all, I owe you for what you did for me."

"What was that?" Shini asked.

Jessica's eyebrows shot up. Josh caught Kiki's eye and tried to beam a message silently into her mind: *Don't break Granny's cover, Kiki! Don't tell Shini about Team O!*

Kiki blushed. "Er...*hai*, of course, for not telling the papers about me and you, Shini...obviously!" Shini laughed, and Kiki turned a secret "oops" face to Josh.

Josh decided he wouldn't tell Granny that their nice quiet afternoon at the football had nearly ended with Kiki revealing their big secret. *That wouldn't go down well at all.*

* * *

The Hanzos' sushi restaurant was a large, upmarket place in Marunouchi, the centre of the Tokyo business district. The area was full of posh restaurants, upmarket hotels and swanky shops. The Hanzos' restaurant was no exception. Josh plucked a maki roll from his plate with his chopsticks and swallowed it nearly whole. He wasn't a big fan of sushi usually, too much slimy fish and chewy rice, but this was incredible – from the way the fish practically melted on his tongue, to the intricate platters that were laid out to look like gardens, with flower beds of sushi rolls and little ponds of soy sauce. He grabbed another roll.

Beside him, Jessica stared around at the walls. They were lined with tanks of colourful fish that sparkled and shimmered as they swam.

Kiki leaned over to fill Josh's cup with green tea, and he remembered that in Japanese restaurants everyone was supposed to fill each others' cups, so he took the square porcelain teapot from her and filled up Kiki's. She gave him a dazzling smile. "Isn't this place great?" she said.

Granny nodded her approval. "It is most civilized," she said.

"And what do you think of the waiter?" Kiki asked, grinning at Jessica as Shini approached their table. He was dressed in a waiter's outfit that was half traditional Japanese and half Western: a white shirt with a black silk jacket and shiny gold buttons.

"Oh, he's okay, I suppose," said Jessica, teasing.

Shini bowed to them all. "May I ask, how do you find your dishes?"

"They're great!" Josh said.

"Indeed, *oishii*," said Granny.

"I hope you didn't mind the photographers outside," Shini said. Josh glanced towards the front of the restaurant. Through the curtain veiling the glass panels in the door and the large, tinted windows, he could make out the shadowy silhouettes of men and women with camera equipment camping on the street outside. They had been there a while. "They are very persistent, especially when Kiki and I are in the same place – they suspect we are an item, but have yet to get the proof. They understand they shouldn't bother people inside my family's restaurant, though."

"A football star working as a waiter," said Jessica. "That would be an amazing photo spread."

"I like to keep my feet on the ground," Shini said. "My parents have supported my career, and out of respect I like to return the favour."

"That is very honourable of you, Shinichiro-san," Granny said with another nod. Josh hoped that Shini knew how much of a compliment that little nod was from stern, serious Granny Murata. She had dressed up for the occasion, though that had only meant exchanging her flowery, light-coloured traditional kimono for a darker one printed with a pattern of golden cranes.

A movement caught his eye at the front door, and he glanced up.

CRASH!

Jessica let out a gasp, and Josh's heart leaped into his throat and seemed to stick there. Shards of glass rained down around them, glinting in the light. The pieces scattered across the floor of the restaurant and Josh felt some striking his head and shoulders.

The large front windows of the restaurant had shattered, and now eight huge men stepped through, their eyes covered by dark glasses. They pulled back their long black coats and drew out aluminium baseball bats.

Diners leaped from their tables, overturning chairs and scattering cushions.

"Hey!" Shini yelled. "What is this?"

"A warning," one of the men growled. The thugs brandished their bats at the diners. Some screamed and threw their arms over their heads, others grabbed their friends' hands and backed away. Granny, Josh and Jessica all sprang to their feet as Kiki dived under one of the tables.

"All of you, get through to the back!" Shini called to the diners, and started to herd the terrified crowd into the kitchen. "I'll call the police!"

As the diners fled, the thugs began to swing their baseball bats wildly, cracking tables and sending shards of glass and china spiralling through the air. One of the goons approached Granny, smacking his bat tauntingly against the palm of his hand. Josh and Jessica took half a step back and Josh watched Granny carefully, waiting for her to take the lead. Whatever she did, they'd be there to back her up.

"Go with the others, old woman," rasped the thug. "This doesn't concern you."

Granny glanced over her shoulder to check that

Shini and the waiters were out of the dining room, and then turned back to the grinning goon. "Are you deaf?" he barked. "I told you—"

Granny's hand was so quick, Josh wasn't sure that she'd actually moved at all. But when he saw the thug drop to his knees, clutching his face, he knew what had happened. Granny had broken his nose with a single blow.

Another thug gave a shout and pointed towards them, and two of his friends thumped across the wooden floor in their direction. One of them tried to tackle Jessica. Josh saw her dodge and turn to plant a hard kick in the middle of his back.

Josh leaped forward, catching the other man on the shoulder with a spinning back kick, but the guy was so solid he barely stumbled. He grabbed Josh by his elbow and swung him against the wall.

"You pathetic weed," the man hissed.

Josh struggled, reaching for the weak point in the thug's grip. It was the first move Granny had taught them, and it always worked – well, almost always. He fumbled it once, before seizing the man's little finger and pulling with all his strength. The thug let go, and Josh pulled his opponent's face down onto his rising knee. The man smacked into his kneecap hard and fell back, crumpling to the floor with his eyes shut.

"Not so pathetic now," Josh muttered. Granny had taught him that good fighting had little to do with strength.

"Josh!" Granny called. He looked round and saw her seize a wooden chair and snap off the legs. She threw one to him, and the other to his sister. Without pausing, Jessica snatched up the weapon, simultaneously punching a goon between the shoulder blades with her other fist. Josh grasped his own chair leg and swung it around, hitting another of the thugs on the side of his head and sending him crashing to the ground.

Kiki's muffled voice sounded from beneath the table. "Yeah, go guys, go!"

Josh dodged between the shattered tables to avoid a thug's lunge, then jabbed his chair leg into his attacker's ribs.

"Oof!" The man doubled over, clutching his side. It was a move Josh had practised in the dojo with a retractable baton, but had never got completely right – until now. He allowed himself a quick fist-pump before the thug was on him again like an enraged gorilla, swinging his baseball bat at Josh's face. Josh backed up, nearly tripping over the splintered remains of a table. He ducked and hopped to avoid another strike, finding himself back-to-back with Jessica, who was aiming a volley of high kicks at another thug.

Josh looked for Granny, and saw her grab one of the men by his shirt collar. She threw him over her shoulder. "Go, Gran—"

"Josh, look out!" Kiki shrieked.

Josh ducked, feeling a *whoosh* as another aluminium bat passed over his head. His foot slipped on the wet, glass-covered floor and he fell backwards. All the breath exploded out of him as his back struck the ground. He gasped and tried to sit up, but before he could, a thug was leaning over him, both hands reaching out to grip his neck.

"Stupid kids!" the thug growled. "I'm going to teach you a lesson!"

Chapter Three

Josh flung his arms up over his face, and the thug's hands closed over his wrists. He brought his knee up into the man's belly, with all the force he could manage.

"Oof!" the thug moaned again, and Josh pressed his advantage, getting in a few rapid kicks to the man's legs. The thug's knees buckled and his grip loosened. Josh managed to slide out from underneath his opponent and get to his feet. He spun, swinging his foot into a roundhouse kick that caught the man on the side of the head with a hard *thwack*. The thug half-collapsed, his eyes rolling back in his head, stunned. Josh could almost see the little cartoon birds circling his head, tweeting in scrawled kanji.

The kitchen door banged open and Shini rushed in, brandishing a huge, heavy-looking soup ladle with both hands. A flood of cooks and waiters streamed out, armed with meat cleavers and frying pans. A man and a woman in late middle age stood behind them, looking fierce.

All the thugs were getting to their feet, groaning and glancing warily in the direction of Granny Murata. She was standing demurely to one side, an innocent old lady once more. The thugs turned and rushed out of the door.

A cheer went up from the cooks and waiters.

"And stay out!" shouted the middle-aged man.

Shini was bending down to help Kiki climb out from underneath her table.

"Are you all right?" he asked. "We managed to get all the customers out through the back, but then I noticed none of you were with them... I worried you might all be..."

"I'm fine!" Kiki said brightly. She threw her arms around him. "Thank goodness you came, we were in real trouble!" she added, giving Josh a wink over Shini's shoulder.

"Quick!" Jessica elbowed Josh, thrusting a vase full of water into his hands. "Help me finish rescuing the fish!"

Josh saw that the thugs had smashed one of the fish tanks. He sprang into action, scooping up a large koi that writhed in his hands, and dropping it into the vase. Soon all the wriggling, flapping fish were safe – if a little bit crowded – and the head waiter took the vases from the twins with a grateful bow.

"Murata-sama, Josh, Jessica," Shini said. He gestured towards the middle-aged couple. "These are my parents, Yoshiro and Chiyoko Hanzo."

Mr. Hanzo came back from the front door and bowed. His hair was grey and he had a large, drooping white moustache. Mrs. Hanzo was a small lady in a black kimono. She wrung her hands together as Granny, Josh and Jessica returned the bow.

"Hanzo-san," Granny said, *"Hajimemashite* – I only wish our meeting could have been a little more peaceful."

Shini's father nodded, frowning. "I too, Murata-sama," he said. His face was red with anger. "What could those thugs want with us?"

"Come on," Jessica said to Josh. "Let's help clear up."

Kiki was already collecting wet, scattered cushions and piling them into a laundry bin. Josh set to checking the furniture for breakages and stacking up chairs. Whenever he crossed the middle of the room he could hear Granny comforting the Hanzos, and he tried to listen in without being noticed.

"They didn't chase after Shini and the guests, or try to make their way to you," Granny was saying. "Frightening as it was, they seemed to be interested only in breaking up the place. I think they wanted to scare you. Has anything like this happened before?"

Josh's Japanese was just about good enough to keep up with the conversation. He may have misheard the odd word, but his granny definitely sounded frightened. *No way was she scared in that attack!*

he thought. What plan was she hatching?

"Never!" Shini's father said.

"Who would want to scare us?" Shini's mother wondered. "For what purpose?"

"Indeed," Granny said. "I am reminded of a time when the Yakuza used tactics just like these to extort money from honest businesses, to 'prevent anything bad happening'. I remember a particularly vile gangster by the name of Yoshida…"

Josh remembered Yoshida, too – in fact, it hadn't been more than two weeks since he'd seen the silver-haired Yakuza boss escaping across the Tokyo rooftops after they'd rescued Kiki from his clutches. Granny had plenty of history with Yoshida, but did she think that this was his doing? Why would he target the Hanzos?

"My grandfather opened this place," said Shini's mother. "He told me a few stories about the Yakuza in his day. But nothing like that has happened here for decades. We've had no threats, and no demands for money." Her husband took her hand and nodded his agreement.

Josh stacked a side table on top of another at the

front of the restaurant so that the floor could be cleared of broken glass. When he looked up there was a gathering crowd on the other side of the smashed windows. A few flashbulbs went off and he reached up to draw the curtains, angrily. The paparazzi had disappeared at the first sign of trouble, but now the thugs had gone they were back for some close-ups. This was bound to make it into the papers, but at least he could stop the paparazzi from getting shots of the Hanzos' upset faces.

As he crossed the restaurant again he met Shini bringing over a mop and bucket. To Josh's surprise, his face crumpled a little.

"I am so sorry about this, Josh," he said quietly.

"Hey, it's not your fault!" Josh reassured him. "Nobody got hurt – and that was down to you getting them out quickly." When this didn't seem to cheer Shini up, he carried on. "We'll come back for another meal when you re-open. So will everyone," he added, wondering if Shini was worried for his parents' business.

"I guess so." Shini shook his head for a second. When he looked up again, he smiled. "Anyway, thank you so much for your help," he said.

"We must repay you," said his father, who had come and taken Shini's mop and bucket from him. "You will all eat for free here any time you wish."

"Oh, thank you!" Jessica said, beaming as she picked her way across the floor, carrying handfuls of chopsticks.

"I think there is something else you might enjoy, too," Shini said, his face lighting up again. "How would you two like to come with me tomorrow to greet the England football team? There is a photo shoot in Ameyoko in the morning, and a welcome reception in the evening."

"Wow!" Josh gasped. He looked at Jessica, who was standing with her mouth open. "That would be amazing!"

"Yes please!" Jessica echoed. "Do...do you think I could interview one or two of the players?" Jessica was a roving reporter for her school newspaper back home, and constantly on the lookout for a fresh story.

Shini grinned at Jessica. "I'm sure I can talk some of my teammates into giving you five minutes."

"Thank you so much for your help," said Mrs. Hanzo, walking up to the twins and bowing low.

"We can finish cleaning up now."

"We didn't mind at all," said Jessica. Mrs. Hanzo gave her a thin, strained smile.

"Indeed, we must be returning home," said Granny. "After all this excitement it will be straight to bed for you two."

Josh and Jessica sighed. Sadly, Josh could tell this wasn't the old lady act – this was their steel-willed grandmother speaking, and she really meant it.

Granny's battered old car threaded its way through the central Tokyo traffic back to the Sakura Apartments in Minato Ward. Flashing lights and white-gloved men and women in peaked caps directed them at junctions. Josh couldn't help grabbing a pencil and taking a ten-second sketch of one of them while they were stopped at an intersection. Even the car journeys in Tokyo seemed to involve a fantastic mix of the traditional and high-tech.

A fire truck crossed the intersection in front of them with its siren wailing.

"Hey, Jess," he said. "Shini said he was going

to call the police, didn't he? How long ago was that?"

Jessica looked at her watch. "About...half an hour before we left? Maybe a bit more..." She raised her eyebrows at him. "The Tokyo police are normally pretty efficient, aren't they?"

"That's what I thought. If it was an emergency – like, a people-are-attacking-my-customers-with-baseball-bats emergency – they should've arrived before we left."

Jessica shrugged. "I s'pose they should. They probably got delayed – it was right in the middle of the business district, the traffic was awful getting there."

"Yeah, I guess," Josh said. But as he watched cars swerve to get out of the fire truck's way, he wasn't so sure. "Granny, why do you think the Hanzos were attacked?"

Granny Murata was silent for a moment. Then she said, "I must admit, I do not know. Nothing they said gave me any clues. I will be sure to keep an eye on the situation, do not worry. Meanwhile, perhaps it is good that you two are to join Shini at this photo shoot tomorrow."

"We'll keep an eye on him," Jessica promised. "And report back to you if we find anything out."

Another mystery, Josh thought. *Don't worry, Mr. and Mrs. Hanzo – the Murata twins are on the case.*

The next morning, Josh frowned out of the car window as Granny pulled up outside what looked like a building site, surrounded by a metal fence.

"Is this really it?" Jessica asked Granny. Granny glanced down at the printout of instructions Shini had emailed them, and nodded.

"*Hai,*" she said. "This is the place."

A security guard in a black cap approached the car.

"*Donata desu ka?*" he asked, peering in. Josh saw that he held a clipboard with a list of names on it.

"Josh and Jessica Murata," Granny answered him.

"Shini Hanzo arranged for us to visit the photo shoot," Jessica said. Josh waited, his heart in his mouth, while the guard scrutinized his list.

Finally he nodded. "*Hai,*" he said. "Come, I will take you."

"Have a nice time, and behave yourselves," Granny

said as Josh and Jessica climbed out of the car. "I will collect you in an hour. And give my best wishes to Shinichiro-san," she added with a piercing glance at Josh.

"Thanks, we will." Josh gave her a nod. Granny had given them strict instructions back in her apartment. Josh had glanced longingly at the bookshelf that held the secret entrance to the team's headquarters, but Granny had been quite firm that there was no need to take any of Team O's super-spy equipment with them. They would be keeping an eye on Shini, nothing more.

Granny drove off, and the guard bowed slightly. He gestured for the twins to follow him through a metal gate and into the construction site.

"Odd place for a photo shoot, isn't it?" Jessica murmured to Josh. As they rounded the corner of a temporary office, the first few floors of a tower block under construction loomed up in front of them, all bare concrete, scaffolding and plastic sheeting blowing in the wind. Actually, Josh thought, it was kind of artistic-looking – in a bleak, urban kind of way. His fingers twitched with the urge to start sketching.

In front of the tower block, there was a large group of people. Most of them were wearing red or white football shirts, bouncing footballs about between them and laughing. Both teams were already here, with officials from the Japanese and English Football Associations in black tracksuits.

"Come on." Jessica prodded Josh forward with the end of her pen. He noticed she'd already got her notebook out and made a few scribbles in her weird shorthand. "Don't freeze up on me now. Look, there's Shini!"

Shini was coming over to greet them, dodging around piles of camera equipment. "Hi guys!" he called. "Come and meet the others." Josh swallowed down his nerves and allowed Shini to steer them into the crowd. "This is Takeshi," Shini said. Josh caught Jessica blushing bright pink – Takeshi Higa's handsome face had grinned down at them from billboards ever since they arrived in Tokyo, as part of the promotion leading up to the match.

"Hi." Josh bowed, then held out his hand, and Takeshi shook it warmly.

"And this is Goro Sasaki, and well, I guess you know Karl Clarke."

Josh found himself looking up at the famous face of the England captain.

"Hello!" He shook Josh's trembling hand. "How are you doing?"

"Um, great, thanks!" Josh couldn't help beaming as he met more and more of the players he'd only ever seen as red and white dots on the television. He tried hard to keep Shini in sight as much as he could, but he started to relax – what could possibly go wrong when they were surrounded by players, managers and security?

Josh turned and bumped into a slight, middle-aged Japanese man in a severe suit and tie, who was standing stiffly amongst the cheery footballers. He stared at Josh.

"Are you supposed to be here?" he asked, in clipped English.

"Yes, we're guests of Shini's," Josh answered. "Josh and Jessica Murata, sir," he added. The man sniffed and bowed formally.

"My name is Kobayashi Kenji. I am the Minister for Social and Cultural Affairs."

"Ah," Josh said.

"*Hajimemashite*, Minister," said Jessica over Josh's shoulder. She had her notepad at the ready. "So…can you tell me why the photo shoot is taking place in this location?"

Kobayashi launched into an explanation at once. "Ah, you see, the tower in progress represents the growing development of Japanese football on the world stage," he said. "The great talent of our players is like the scaffolding on which we hang international renown for our whole country, just as Japan is thriving in the realms of culture, tourism and business."

He broke off and looked at his watch. Perhaps he had a meeting to get to, Josh thought.

"Ah, the photographer is here," Kobayashi continued, indicating a young man dressed in black who was unpacking and setting up equipment. A grumpy frown passed across the Minister's face. "You will kindly not interfere, and don't touch anything."

"*Hai*," said Josh and Jessica together. Josh spotted two metal, folding chairs that looked like they weren't in the way, and the twins sat down on them, watching the photographer and his assistant eagerly as they got to work.

The assistant ran back and forth, helping the footballers to feel at ease and getting them to pull a bunch of fantastic poses: kicking the football, leaping in the air, even swinging off the scaffolding.

"Don't you dare pull a muscle, Gallagher!" the England manager yelled as the defender jumped down onto the platform with a thump and a hearty laugh.

Josh pulled out his sketchpad and began to draw as fast as he could, trying to capture the best poses.

Takeshi and Jamie Elton began an epic, highly competitive game of keepy-uppy, with the photographer snapping away gleefully. In the end it was Takeshi who dropped the ball, earning playful jeers from his teammates and a great round of applause from everyone for both players. The only person not clapping was Kobayashi. Josh frowned. He found himself sketching the Minister, trying to capture his weird, uptight pose and the glint off his watch as he looked at it yet again. Underneath he scrawled the words, *What is his problem?* He showed the drawing to Jessica, who sniggered.

"All right," the photographer called. "Everyone in for a big group shot please."

Both teams crowded onto the platform. Josh settled down to shade one of his sketches, with half an eye on the players.

"What is he doing?" Jessica muttered.

"Who?" Josh asked. Jessica pointed to the platform. Kobayashi was now up there with the players, arranging them in position.

"Okay, big smiles..." the photographer called out. Josh glanced at Kobayashi as he backed away from the platform. Something had caught Josh's eye – it was that watch again, gleaming in the sunlight as Kobayashi glanced at it. Then Josh saw his eyes flick up – way up, past the platform, up to the top of the half-constructed building. Josh looked up too.

Was that...something moving? Josh frowned.

Clang!

A dark object bounced into the air. At first it was just a black shape in the sky, but it fell fast, clattering off scaffold poles and splintering through wooden boards. Josh's heart felt like it had frozen in his chest. It was a huge block of cement!

"Look out!" Jessica screamed, pointing upwards. Josh sprang out of his chair as if it was on fire.

"Move!" he shouted. "Now!"

Shini and the others glanced up, shock and fear welling up in their faces.

The photographer and assistant grabbed their cameras and ran back. There wasn't time to do anything but dive out of the way.

Smash! The block crashed into a scaffold full of tools and sent them scattering.

It was still falling.

Josh felt as if cold water had been poured down the back of his neck – Shini was still on the platform.

I said I'd watch him. Now I'm going to watch him get squashed. He started forward, madly. Shini and Goro dived headfirst off the platform, just as the concrete block smashed into the centre of it with a great *thud*, splintering the surface.

Josh's ears were still ringing as he ran forward and took Shini's arm, helping him to his feet.

"Are you okay? Is everyone all right?" he asked. The players edged forward again, stunned, and crowded around the ruined platform. A cloud of brick dust and splinters blew away on the breeze and they brushed themselves down as they stared at the concrete block embedded in the wood where they'd just been standing.

"No injuries, I think," Shini said. He let out a long, relieved sigh.

"Well, that was..." Josh began.

Twang! Clang!

He looked up. A pneumatic drill was ricocheting down the tower, twisting chaotically. It bounced off the scaffolding and scythed out into the air, its sharp metal edge glinting in the light, hurtling right towards the players.

Chapter Four

The drill seemed to fall in slow motion, heavy, sharp…
and deadly.

Jessica was grabbing players by the arms and
dragging them out of the way, but they were moving
too slowly – Josh had to do something, *anything*…

His eye fell on the concrete block. He gasped in a
breath and leaped up, planting one foot on the block
and using it to launch himself higher into the air. He
brought up his foot as he flew, spinning at the last

second and thrusting a flying kick at the drill. If he missed, it was all over.

The world seemed to slow down, and then he landed a kick on the side of the drill handle and it spun away, thudding harmlessly into the mud a couple of metres from the players. Josh hit the ground next to it and skidded.

He looked up to find Jessica and the players arranged in a circle around him, gazing down at Josh in amazement. Karl Clarke helped him to his feet.

"That was incredible," Clarke said. "You just saved our lives!" Josh swallowed hard, then grinned as everyone swarmed forward to shake his hand.

"Both of you did," Goro Sasaki said, bowing to Jessica and then scooping her up into a big hug. "If you hadn't warned us we'd never have got out of the way in time!"

Josh looked around for Shini. He was fine, but standing by himself, staring up at the tower, his face pale. Josh was about to go over to him when one of the Japanese FA officials pushed past Josh and Jessica, waving his arms furiously.

Josh watched him stomp through the crowd to

where the Minister for Social and Cultural Affairs was standing staring at the devastation, his face as white as the handkerchief pressed to his sweating forehead. The official reeled off a long stream of complaints in Japanese as he came face-to-face with Kobayashi.

Takeshi saw him watching the exchange.

"He's saying he is...er...disappointed," he translated diplomatically. "The site was supposed to have been checked, so accidents like this couldn't happen. Kobayashi could get into a lot of trouble for this."

"Thank goodness nobody was hurt!" said Jessica.

"But they could have been," Josh said quietly. He glanced at the platform again, at the huge block of concrete still embedded in its splintered, wooden surface. He turned so that only Jessica could hear him. "That looks really heavy, doesn't it? You'd have to give it a pretty hard shove if you wanted it to move – or fall."

Jessica raised an eyebrow. "You don't think..." she whispered, "...that maybe it wasn't an accident?"

Josh chewed his lip. "I thought I saw something

moving up there before it fell. I don't know what it was, just a dark shape – it caught my eye and then it was gone."

"Should we tell someone?" Jessica suggested. "After all, we were meant to be keeping an eye on Shini."

"I dunno. I've got a bad feeling." First the attack on the Hanzos' restaurant, and now this... Could there be a connection? He shook his head. "It's possible it was an accident. We need to know more. Let's keep quiet for now. I think we should keep watch for anything else suspicious."

Jessica nodded. "Right. Let's go over what happened later, so my notes are totally accurate if it turns out to be important."

When Josh looked around again the shoot was in disarray, the officials hurrying their players back to the team coaches.

"Where's Shini?" Jessica said. "I was going to tell him we'd see him at the reception." She frowned. "I know he wasn't hurt, but I hope he's okay..."

Josh looked round at the spot where Shini had been standing. "He must have got on the coach," he said, watching the team bus pulling away and out of the gate.

As the coaches drove out, a large black car drove in. *That must be the Minister's ride,* he thought. *And there he goes. Looks like he can't wait to get out of here.*

Kobayashi was making a beeline for the car. He passed a blue jacket that had been left draped over the back of a chair and stopped, as if he might pick it up, but he was just bending down to tie his shoelace. He walked on and climbed into the car.

Obviously thinks he's too important to deal with lost property, Josh thought.

Josh walked over to the jacket as the shiny black car drove back out through the gate. Jessica followed. He picked it up and showed it to her.

"I wonder who left this behind," he said. "We should find someone to give it to."

"Looks like a Team Japan jacket. If it's one of the players' we can give it back this evening," Jessica pointed out. "Has it got a name?"

"Oh – it's Shini's." Josh stared at the name sewn on the inside of the lapel. "He really must've been in a hurry."

"Hey," said Jessica, bending to pick something up. It was a piece of card. "This fell out. Could be a business card, or..." She turned it over, and her face froze. Josh felt a shiver pass over the back of his neck.

"What? Jess, what?" He took the card out of her hand. There was a single line of spidery writing on the other side. It read: *Next time we won't miss.*

Jessica looked up at Josh, her eyes wide. "I guess that answers our question," she gulped. "It *wasn't* an accident."

"Yeah," Josh said. "And it has something to do with Shini."

"So it must be connected to the Hanzos' restaurant getting smashed up too," Jessica said, almost to herself. "But why? What's going on?"

"No idea." Josh looked up as Granny's car pulled into the construction site. "But I know who we need to go to next."

Josh turned the piece of card over and over in his fingers as they rode the secret elevator from Granny's flat, deep down into the hidden basement beneath the Sakura Apartments. He knew now that there was somebody after Shini – he only hoped Team Obaasan could help them figure out who, and why.

The whole team was waiting for them, relaxing in the soft leather chairs. Nana, the team's surveillance expert, was serving steaming green tea from a stainless-steel and porcelain teapot. She balanced her own cup on the edge of the control panel, making tech-expert Mimasu wince. Mr. Nakamura, the ancient Team O medic, and Mr. Yamamoto were bent over a touch-screen pad, in the middle of a virtual game of Go, a traditional board game that looked a bit like solitaire. Josh smiled to himself – it reminded him of the OAP community centre his English grandparents visited sometimes, but with a lot more weapons and fewer floral-patterned sofas.

Mr. Yamamoto raised his cup in greeting as the twins walked in. "Ah Josh-kun, Jessica-chan. Mimi-san says you have a case for us."

"We might have," Josh said. Nana passed a cup to Granny, who blew on her hot tea before taking a sip. Josh took a deep breath. "We think something dangerous might be going on. Something to do with Shinichiro Hanzo."

"The football player?" Mr. Nakamura asked, raising his bushy grey eyebrows.

"First – I think Granny told you – there was the attack on his parents' restaurant last night," Josh began. "It was like someone wanted to scare them, to damage the place but not actually hurt anyone. Then this morning someone nearly *was* hurt." He described the "accident" at the photo shoot.

"Thank goodness you two were not harmed!" Sachiko gasped.

"Indeed," said Granny. She was staring into the middle distance, her eyes unfocused for a moment. Was she imagining what she would've done if they had been hurt? How would she have explained it to their parents?

"Then afterwards we found this," Jessica said, nodding at Josh.

Josh passed the card around the team. "It was in Shini's jacket. It must have been planted there while nobody was looking."

"In fact," Jessica said, flipping through her notebook,

"there was something else as well. Remember when we first met Shini? There was a man in the changing room. Shini said he was a weird fan, but maybe there was more to it than that."

"That could have been his first warning," said Sachiko, stroking her wrinkled chin thoughtfully. "Or our villain making some sort of demand."

"Money, do you think?" Nana asked.

"Straightforward extortion? I think not," Granny said, taking a sip of tea. "I would have believed it after the restaurant – but someone could truly have been injured at the photo shoot today. I imagine whoever we're looking for really wanted something bad to happen, and with the sabotage at Shini's restaurant, I wonder if he's the person the attackers wanted to get at."

"But who would want to hurt Shini Hanzo?" Nana frowned.

"Nobody who cares about Japanese football, that's for certain," Josh said. "Not with the England game coming up."

"Then a personal rivalry?" Jessica wondered. "Something…girlfriend-related?" She looked at Josh.

He hadn't thought of that – could it be about Kiki? Either one of them could have a jealous ex, or an insane fan who felt threatened. He shook his head.

"Shini and...and his girlfriend haven't gone public yet," he said, just managing to avoid mentioning Kiki. "So it'd have to be someone *really* close to them, and..." A thought struck him. "Wait, there's something else. This could be about the big game itself."

"Shinichiro's contribution will be invaluable on Saturday, won't it?" Nana said. "Nobody who wants Japan to stand a chance against England would let him come to harm."

"But what if someone wants them to lose?" Jessica said, her eyes widening. "What if – no, not someone on the England team, surely?"

Josh shook his head. "They got on so well at the photo shoot. And all of them were on the ground with us, even the managers. *And* they hadn't arrived in the country when we saw the man in the changing rooms yesterday."

"Well if it's not someone connected with the team, some mad England fan?" Jessica suggested, wincing.

"No...I can't believe that," Josh said. He tried to

sound certain, but he felt his face flush with shame at the very idea.

"Ah..." said Mr. Yamamoto, quietly. The rest of Team O turned to look at him. He was staring at the frozen game of Go on the pad in front of him. "I think it may come down to money, after all."

"You have a theory, Yamamoto-san?" Granny asked.

Mr. Yamamoto stood up and walked to the console. After pressing a few buttons, the banks of screens filled up with Japanese websites.

"Betting websites. Let's see..." He scrolled through them, scanning the columns of figures. "This reminds me of a scam I came across in the forties – but on a larger scale, *much* larger...yes, indeed," he said, pointing out some of the kanji. "The odds on the match have changed again, and they are even more strongly in Japan's favour since we spoke about them yesterday. Everyone has been putting money on them to win the match. But if you put money on England to win, with these odds...and if, say, the star goalkeeper of Japan were to let in a few goals, or be mysteriously injured just before the match..."

"Then if someone bet just one hundred yen on England..." Mimasu said, rising to join Mr. Yamamoto at the console, her eyes flicking over the numbers on the betting websites. Josh guessed she was doing some complicated maths in her head. "They could make...*millions*."

Mr. Yamamoto turned to Granny, who nodded.

"I believe we have our motive," she said. "And a fix on this scale is certainly government business. Team O will take up the investigation."

Josh let out a long breath. "There's something else," he said. "We didn't see any police cars last night at the restaurant. Shini said he'd phone them, but..."

"I'll check," said Nana, turning and tapping her control pad. One of the screens filled with long strings of numbers and she scanned them as they scrolled past. "No," she said. "I see no call to the police from the restaurant yesterday."

"Why wouldn't he call them?" Jessica asked.

"Perhaps the mysterious gambler warned him against it – he could have threatened to hurt Shini, or his parents, if Shini went to the police."

"We had better tread carefully," said Mr. Nakamura. "If they find out we're on the case they might think Shini has called us in and do something even more drastic."

"I'll put out a protection call on the Hanzos," Nana said. "Other field agents will keep an eye on them until we have discovered the source of the threat."

"And how do we do that?" Jessica asked. "Plenty of people would be interested in making millions on a bet. It isn't much to go on."

"We need to find another lead," Granny said. She finished her tea, set the cup down in its saucer decisively and turned to Josh and Jessica. "You two will attend the reception this evening as planned – but now you will be there on business, not pleasure. Be on your guard for threats against Shini, and look out for anything that might be a clue. I don't want you to take unnecessary risks," she added sternly. Josh thought she might've seen the gleam in his eye at the thought of officially working for Team O again. He couldn't help it. He'd be attending a posh reception to stop a possible international gambling fix!

Granny went on, "We must find out who is

responsible for this, and soon – it's already Wednesday, so we have two full days to make sure that Shini is safe and gets to the match on Saturday. You will have remote backup from the team, in case anything goes wrong." She nodded at Mimasu, who nodded back and headed towards her workshop.

"I'll bring out the latest," Mimasu muttered as she disappeared through the doorway.

Josh exchanged glances with Jessica, who looked just as excited as he was. He could guess what "the latest" meant – *secret-agent gadgets*. James Bond had nothing on the Murata family!

Even though he was worried for Shini, Josh couldn't help a bubble of excitement rising in his chest. He and his sister were about to become government agents for the second time in as many weeks. Scary, but on the other hand, he thought...*I can't wait!*

Chapter Five

"Does it look okay?" Jessica asked. She gave Josh a twirl as the lift swished up towards the fancy bar on the twenty-seventh floor of the Shangri-La Hotel. She was wearing a blue embroidered silk shirt and a black skirt.

Josh shrugged. "There are about a billion mirrors in this lift," he pointed out. "But yeah, very pretty, I suppose."

Jessica rolled her eyes at him. "I *mean*, can you

see where I've got my radio mic hidden in my collar? You're lucky, it's not so difficult to hide kit in a posh suit."

"That's certainly true," said Mr. Yamamoto's voice in Josh's ear. *"I once smuggled eighteen swords out from under the nose of the Black Fist Gang, under cover of a Venetian ball. And I still had time to dance with the Grand Duke's wife, and – oh, all right, Mimi. Perhaps that is a story for another time."*

Josh smiled as he imagined the frosty expression on Granny's face. With Mimasu's amazing invisible ear-buds it felt as if Team O were standing right beside him. Josh looked himself up and down in the mirror. His suit was a sort of greyish-black, and ridiculously swanky. Last time he checked, he was a wannabe comic book artist from North London, not some kind of ambassador. He wondered if all secret agents felt this weird the first time they wore a tuxedo.

"Good luck, kids." It was Sachiko's voice. *"Don't forget to use your secret cameras if you need to get a record of anything."*

"We won't," Josh and Jessica replied. Josh lifted his watch to eye-level and pointed the practically sub-atomic camera in its side at one of the mirrors, catching a good shot of him and Jessica standing side by side in their finery.

"One for the holiday album," he joked.

The lift opened, and they gave their names to a uniformed doorman, who waved them through into the Welcome Reception.

The players were all there, dressed in suits that were even smarter than Josh's, with crisp lines and expensive-looking clips on their ties. A few of the Japanese players wore suits that looked like a fusion of Eastern and Western styles, with bright silk prints and thin black neckties. There were a lot more people too, women dressed in elegant cocktail dresses or traditional embroidered kimonos, waiters, and journalists with blue security badges on their lapels.

Josh looked around for Shini, and spotted him standing below a large, beautiful painting of snow-capped mountains breaking through a cloud. He was chatting to the England manager and one of the journalists. He looked quite cheerful, and this place did seem safe – there were several security guards on the doors, and the twins had had to be given a special key to even get the elevator to stop at the right floor. Still, Josh made sure to keep Shini in sight as much as possible as they milled around the party.

The reception was in full swing. The players had obviously got over the shock of this morning and they were laughing and joking together again, under the appreciative eyes of the various officials, important businessmen and journalists.

"Go on," Takeshi Higa was saying, as he gave Jamie Elton an encouraging grin. "Do it like I taught you."

"*Ha...hajimey...ma...shayter*," Elton said, bowing low to one of the journalists, who roared with laughter.

"*Hajimemashite*," he said, bowing back. The group of people they were standing with all smiled and laughed...except for one man. *Kobayashi*.

Josh's eyes narrowed. "Hey Jess, look," he said, tapping her on the shoulder.

"He doesn't look any more comfortable, does he?" Jessica said, turning to glance at the Minister.

Kobayashi was bowing and shaking the hand of the England manager, but he still looked really stiff.

There was something about him, Josh thought, the way his eyes scanned the room, as if he was looking for someone, but couldn't see them.

"As if he was looking for someone..." he repeated aloud, under his breath.

"Huh?" Jessica asked.

"It's just...this morning, I first saw the concrete block because I was watching Kobayashi, and his eyes flicked up. I think he looked up...before it fell," he whispered.

"Are you sure?" Jessica looked at Kobayashi again, her eyes wide with suspicion.

"Not a hundred per cent. But...maybe ninety-five per cent."

"That's quite a lot of per cent," Jessica murmured.

"Even if he just saw something moving before I did," Josh went on, the pieces sliding together in his head, "I didn't hear him call out or try to move anyone. Did you?"

Jessica shook her head. "Not after it fell... But before, remember, he was rearranging the players?"

"Of course!"

Josh wanted to smack his hand to his forehead,

and only just stopped himself when he felt the weight of the secret camera around his wrist. *Incognito, remember?*

"Mr. Yamamoto," he whispered, pretending to scratch his ear so he could tap the ear-bud to make sure it was working. It buzzed. "Are you there?"

"*We're here, Josh,*" Mr. Yamamoto said. "*We hear you. Mimasu-san is checking out your Minister Kobayashi's government records as we speak. Keep an eye on him.*"

"*Hai,*" Josh whispered. "Come on, let's get closer. I have stuff I can ask the manager as a cover." They made their way through the crowd, navigating by the distinctive blond hair of one of the footballers, but when they arrived in the place where Kobayashi had been standing, he had already gone.

"Argh," Jessica said under her breath. "Lost him."

"*Nana-san,*" Mr. Yamamoto's voice rang in Josh's ear. "*Take a look at the CCTV, where has Minister Kobayashi gone to?*"

"*That's him,*" said Mimasu. "*The tall, fragile-looking one.*"

"*He's left the room – he's out in one of the service corridors,*" said Nana's voice. "*Through the door beside the bar. There's a...*" The voice cut out.

What? Josh thought, holding his breath. *There's a what?*

Jessica raised her hand as if to play with her hair, and tapped her earphone.

"Hello?" she whispered.

"*...waiter, he's...*" Nana's voice came back, and immediately went away again. "*...food on a tray. They're having...not happy at all. Something about the food...*"

Josh swallowed. "If you can hear us, Mimasu-san, there's something wrong with the earpieces," he whispered. He turned to look for the door beside the bar, and his throat tightened. A waiter had just entered the room through the door, carrying a plate of food. Kobayashi was nowhere to be seen – was he still in the back corridor? Josh watched the waiter walk across the room. The other waiters glided across the carpeted floor like dancers, but this man stomped. He was big, wearing a waistcoat that didn't do up completely across his chest...and he was making a beeline straight for a small group of players – among them Takeshi...and Shini.

"Come on!" Jessica hissed. They dodged back through the crowd as the waiter approached Shini's corner of the room.

"Delicious canapés," Josh heard the waiter say as they drew closer. "You must try one, Hanzo-sama."

Josh ducked under a player's arm and around a woman in a black dress, longing to shout a warning – but how could he explain what was going on? He just had to get to Shini, to stop him taking the food...

"Team O, come in!" Jessica whispered frantically behind him. "Can you hear us, Granny? We need you!" Panic made her voice tremble, but Josh hadn't time to panic, he just had to get to Shini...

"Ooh," Takeshi grinned. "Looks good!" He snatched the little circle of bread and paté that Shini was reaching for, and tossed it into his mouth. He started to chew, crumbs falling from his lips. He swallowed hard and reached for another appetizer. Soon he'd eaten three or four, his cheeks red. His cheeks were *too* red... Then a crease appeared in his brow. His smile froze on his face and he bent over in a violent coughing fit. Josh pushed past a couple of journalists to run to Takeshi's side. He was clutching at his throat, his eyes wide with fear.

"Takeshi? What's wrong?" Shini was saying. He grabbed hold of Takeshi, who was coughing hard, his knees buckling. Josh looked around for the waiter. He was already making a run for it, dropping the canapé tray to the floor and pushing through the bemused crowd before they realized what was happening.

"Takeshi's been...something's happened," Jessica said. Josh saw her remember their cover and clench her teeth over the word "poisoned" halfway through the sentence. "He needs an ambulance!"

"*Kkkkkksssssssshhhh...*" Josh winced as a static crackling hissed into his ear. "*Nakamura-san will... don't let the waiter get...*"

Shini stared at Jessica, then plunged his hands into his pockets and pulled out a mobile phone. "Is there a doctor here?" he called out to the assembled, shocked guests. He tapped a number into his phone, but the signal was weak.

"We'll, um, go and ask at reception," Jessica

improvised. "Come on!" She grabbed Josh's arm and they dodged out of the crowd that was forming around Shini and Takeshi. As they passed a waitress, she paused and Josh nearly ran into Jessica's back. "Can someone call an ambulance? One of the players is really ill."

The waitress's eyes widened as she saw Takeshi doubled up. She nodded and ran towards the main doors.

"Come on. We can't let that waiter get away," Jessica hissed to Josh, as they started pushing through the crowds again.

They were just in time to see the man yank open the door behind the bar. Josh swallowed hard, and put on a burst of speed. If anything serious happened to Takeshi...

The twins pushed past the stunned bar manager, and slammed open the door that the waiter had gone through. The short corridor beyond was obviously not a visitor area, with its bare plaster walls and faint smell of dishwashers. It was empty, but they could hear echoing footsteps, getting fainter.

"We're following the waiter," Josh said, hoping

Team O could hear him. He and Jessica sprinted to the other end of the corridor. The only door was marked *Fire Exit*, and Josh pushed it open to find himself in a cold, brightly lit stairwell. Tiled stairs led both up and down, with a black metal banister between them and a long drop down to the ground floor. Josh stopped and held his breath, listening. The footsteps were still sounding, somewhere below them.

"He's heading down the fire exit," Josh whispered.

"Oh, good, stairs again," Jessica sighed, leaning on the black metal banister and looking down. Josh took a deep breath. The last time they'd chased a crook down a flight of stairs, they'd had to be rescued by Granny. This time, she probably had no idea where they were.

"I don't think he's heard us," Josh whispered. He motioned Jessica to follow him as quickly and quietly as she could. Josh moved forward down the stairs, still listening out for the footsteps of the waiter. It sounded like he wasn't running – his footsteps were slow and even.

The sign for floor eighteen passed by, then floor seventeen. As they passed the door to floor sixteen

Jessica stopped dead. Josh turned to look at her, his eyebrows raised. *What?* Jessica tugged her ear. Josh listened, and heard...nothing. The footsteps had stopped. *No!* The waiter was getting away. Josh launched into a run, two steps at a time, kicking off the wall at the turn of the stairs.

"Josh!" Jessica cried, and Josh looked up just in time to see a huge figure looming into his field of vision, fist first.

The waiter had been hiding just around the corner. Josh threw up his arms as the punch hit him, and fell back hard onto his elbows, trying to swallow a cry of pain as his bones smacked into the stairs.

The waiter vaulted over Josh, his big boots smacking down on the landing above.

"Think I'm stupid?" the waiter demanded. "Think I don't know when I'm being followed?"

Josh sat up, his head spinning and his arms covered in burning bruises. He got to his feet and charged back up the steps. The waiter was busy fighting Jessica on the landing, blocking her kicks with one arm and reaching for her hair with the other. Josh leaped, aiming a high side kick to the back of the man's head. As he hurtled through the air he saw Jessica's foot coming up in a plunging front kick – they'd meet in the middle of the man's head. No way he'd be walking away from that...

Except that the waiter ducked. Josh winced as their feet slammed together in midair. Their knees buckled, Josh crumpled to the floor, the sole of his foot aching worse than a thousand wasp stings.

Josh tried to get to his feet, but fell back again, his leg twitching nastily when he tried to put his weight on it. The man seized Jessica and threw her against the banister. Josh watched helplessly as she hit the metal rail and tipped over it head first.

Josh reached out to grab her skirt, but the fabric slipped through his fingers.

With a scream, Jessica fell.

Chapter Six

"Jess!" Josh yelled, springing to his feet despite the pain. Jessica twisted and her hand slapped down on the metal banister. She held on tight, dangling over sixteen floors of gaping space. One of her shoes slipped off and clattered all the way down to the bottom, bouncing noisily off the banisters on the way.

The waiter was already racing away, down the stairs.

"Help!" gasped Jessica.

"Hang on," Josh said, reaching over the banister with both hands. "I've got you." Jessica grasped his arm with her free hand and he pulled her up, her feet scrambling to get a toe-hold on the stairs and metal railing. His arm ached, but he managed to grab her under her other arm and finally she toppled back over to safety.

"You okay?" Josh asked.

"That was too close," Jessica said. "Yes. Yes, I'm fine – but he's getting away!"

Josh peered over into the stairwell. The waiter was a few floors down. Jessica got to her feet, limped a few steps and then started running. Josh ran after her. The bite of the bruising on his foot was hurting him less now, and he thought that the waiter was slowing as they reached level ten, seven, three, minus one...

They got to the bottom of the stairs, totally out of breath, and Josh fell on the fire exit, stumbling through as it opened.

Beyond, there was a basement car park – an enormous dingy space full of gleaming limousines and zippy hybrids belonging to the residents of the hotel.

Josh looked around, his heart sinking right into his boots. There was no sign at all of the waiter…only the distant roar of a car engine.

Jessica looked out into the car park, shook her head and leaned heavily against the wall. "Oh…*fine*," she gasped. "Go ahead and run. That's just…*fine*. Cheater."

Josh glanced at the door, which he was still holding open. A large sign read: *Alarm Will Sound When Door Is Opened*; a couple of cut wires were hanging out just beneath it.

"What now?" Jessica asked.

"I guess we…go back. Find out if Takeshi's okay. Meet up with Team O and make our report."

"All right," Jessica sighed, and she went back to the stairwell to retrieve her shoe. "But let's take the lift back up, okay? I think I've had enough of stairs for one lifetime."

As the twins emerged from the lift they found Takeshi looking very ill, being wheeled out of the bar on a stretcher. An elderly doctor was talking to the players and journalists, who had all gathered around the doorway, looking horrified. Shini's eyes were still wide, and Jamie Elton was chewing on his knuckle. "He'll be all right now," said the doctor. "He might even play on Saturday. We'll do our best."

The doctor turned and gave Josh a wink as they got out of the lift to make room for the stretcher. Josh did a double-take. It was Mr. Nakamura, Team O's medical expert.

"No sign of our friend Kobayashi," Mr. Nakamura whispered. "He's made a run for it. Mimasu says she's sorry about the technology failure, something to do with navigating hotel security."

Josh gave a tiny hand-wave, as if to say *No big deal. Yeah, no worries, my heart may never be the same, but apart from that, we're good*, he thought.

"Anyway, I think this party's wrapping up." Mr. Nakamura twitched a smile at Josh and Jessica. "See you at HQ in a couple of hours."

Josh watched the banks of computer screens as Nana tapped away at her control panel, bringing up everything they had on Minister Kobayashi.

"It's not much," she said. "Barely more than you

could find out with an internet search engine. Middle class family, graduated from university – he was treasurer of the Musical Theatre Society, but they kicked him out for being too tight with the finances. He got a job in the civil service, and then went into politics." She scrolled through more data. "These government emails show he is not exactly well-liked, but no more than that. There's not even a hint of corruption."

"Could we have the wrong man?" Jessica asked. Mimasu shook her head.

"Absolutely not. The footage we have from the corridor before Takeshi was poisoned clearly shows him standing with the waiter, pointing to the poisoned canapés. He is certainly behind these attacks on Shini."

"But we have no motive, other than a sudden desire to get rich quick," said Sachiko.

"Perhaps," Nana said, turning away from the screens to look at Granny, "we should change tack. We only have two more days – that may not be enough to catch Kobayashi and get him to confess. But we might be able to find out more through other channels.

If it's a gambling scam, a trip to Shinjuku might be in order."

"Why Shinjuku?" Jessica asked.

"It is the gambling hub of all Japan," said Sachiko. "There are several gambling houses in the area – both legal and...not so legal. They are a known hangout of many Yakuza; where they spend their ill-gotten yen."

"Indeed," Granny nodded. "A good idea, Nana-san. I will take a trip to the Omajinai. It is my favourite gambling den, the most disreputable I know. If crooked gambling on this scale is taking place, somebody there will know about it."

Josh blinked. Had his granny really just said the words "my favourite gambling den"? Just yesterday she was condemning all gambling, calling it filthy! He glanced at Jessica, who was staring at Granny with her mouth hanging slightly open.

"Well – we're ready to go," Jessica said. "Whatever we need to do to keep Shini safe..."

Granny shook her head. "You may ride in the surveillance van with the team, but the Omajinai is no place for children." Josh blinked again. The way she frowned and pursed her lips – exactly like the straight-laced grandmother they'd known until this holiday, and not at all like someone who knew enough gambling dens to have a favourite. *Will I ever get used to Granny Murata's contradictions?* he wondered.

Josh had been a bit sceptical when he first saw the old off-white van with the grimy ladder fixed on top. But behind the blacked-out windows there was a small surveillance console, a flat screen, racks of headphones, ear-buds and microphones, and enough comfy chairs for Josh, Jessica and all of Team O.

As they drove through Shinjuku, Josh blinked out of the tinted windows at the sheer number of neon signs and flashing lights. Apparently this was a hotspot for bars and nightclubs, as well as dodgy gambling dens.

The Omajinai was a Chinese gambling house on a quieter backstreet. The van parked around the corner in an alleyway and Granny climbed out, moving as if she was a frail old lady.

Nana pulled her chair up to the console, a pair of

enormous headphones totally covering the sides of her small head. Her fingers danced across the buttons and slides, while her eyes stayed fixed on the screen showing the CCTV feed from outside. The camera whirred around at her command and focused on the dingy entrance to the Omajinai gambling den.

It was pretty low-key, by Shinjuku standards. It had a plain grey front door, and no windows Josh could see. The door was flanked by two decorative bushes and two large Chinese men with their hair slicked back in ponytails. They opened the door for Granny, and one of them patted her up and down, searching her for weapons. Jessica gasped and shot Mr. Nakamura a shocked look.

"It's all right," Mr. Nakamura said. "They will find nothing – she is wearing only her ear-bud and microphone, and they are too small to be detected."

"No camera?" Josh asked. "No weapons? *Nothing*?"

Mr. Nakamura shook his head. "Mimi-san will arm herself, if the need arises, but the plan is simply to stay incognito and gather information. For visuals, we will have to rely on the place's own security cameras."

Mimasu raised a hand, as if to say *I'm on it*. She was beside Nana, tapping furiously into a laptop while endless strings of text scrolled by. About twenty minutes passed in near-silence, with only the occasional word from Granny coming over their headphones.

"If only the passwords for the Omajinai surveillance feeds were as easy to hack as the ones for the civic CCTV cameras..." Mimasu sighed, stretching her fingers out with a chorus of little arthritic clicks. "I'll have it in a second."

"Chow," said Granny's voice in Josh's ear. It was accompanied by the clacking of tile counters being moved around on a wooden table. Josh supposed that after the gambling revelation, he shouldn't be surprised by anything Granny did. Not even speaking perfect Mandarin and playing mah-jong like a pro. He knew the game involved picking up little painted tiles from an elaborate layout, and putting them down again. Beyond that, it was a mystery.

"Ah!" Mimasu exclaimed. "There it is. Nana-san, I'm passing you the codes now."

The screen flickered and changed to a black and white view of a cavernous, smoke-filled room inside the Omajinai. There were a few banks of slot machines, and a long bar in the middle. Most of the space was taken up by dozens of small square tables, most of them set up for mah-jong matches, with four players sitting around each table. Spectators and gamblers milled around, drinking at the bar or watching matches.

Granny spoke again, a string of Mandarin words Josh couldn't even begin to follow, and laid down her hand of mah-jong tiles with a series of smug little clicks. Josh searched for the movement on the screen, and finally spotted her. She was at a table near the bottom left-hand corner. From the way she scooped chips into a neat pile, and the furiously jealous expressions on the faces of the three Chinese ladies she was playing against, Josh guessed she'd just won. A spectator clapped politely and moved on to a different table.

A young lady in a slim-fitting red kimono shuffled up to their table, bowed, and started to reset the tiles for a new game. Granny poured a new cup of tea for the lady on her right, with an innocent smile that made her opponents frown even harder. Josh noticed that her pile of chips was twice the size of all theirs put together.

"You should probably lose this hand, Mimi-san," Mr. Yamamoto said, looking over Josh's shoulder. "Or those ladies will make a scene!"

"They do look about ready to attack you with their purses," Sachiko added, laughing.

"I hope not, for their sake," said Jessica. "They don't know what they're getting into with Granny."

On screen, they saw Granny raise her hand, apparently scratching her head. There were two soft *thunk* sounds. She'd tapped her ear-bud, twice to indicate *yes*. She didn't look happy about it though.

As the four ladies scooped up their new tiles, Granny spoke again, another stream of Mandarin.

"She has mentioned the football game," Mr. Yoshida translated.

"You don't think those women could have anything to do with the scheme?" Jessica frowned, staring at the little old ladies.

"No," said Nana. "But she has shown her interest in the subject. Look at the men at the table behind her."

Josh peered at the screen. At the table Nana was pointing to, four young men with slicked-back hair, wearing shiny suits – Josh thought one of them might've actually been made of leather – were gambling with four enormous piles of gaming chips.

"Almost certainly, those are young Yakuza," Nana explained. "Newly rich, and foolish with money by the way they gamble. In a while, Mimi-san will talk about going to a sporting bookmakers and placing a bet on Japan to win the game on Saturday. If one of them knows about the match fixing, he may not be able to resist gloating to the harmless old woman, just a little. It would be enough for her to know she's on the right track."

"Does that work?" Josh asked, astonished.

"More often than you'd think," Mr. Nakamura said, with a wink. "Many older Yakuza are wise and cunning, but the young ones are frequently foolhardy."

"On the other hand," Mimasu said, "we may not have to wait for that. Look who has just arrived."

On the screen, a figure was standing in the doorway. The young woman in the kimono was taking his coat. He looked around and coughed, obviously uncomfortable in the disreputable surroundings.

"Kobayashi!" Josh gasped.

"That pretty much proves he's guilty, right?" Jessica asked Mr. Yamamoto. He narrowed his eyes.

"It is certainly a good indication. Do you see him, Mimi-san?"

Granny's ear-bud gave another two soft *thunks* for "yes". Josh watched as the young woman escorted Kobayashi between the tables, right to the back of the room, and...Josh leaned in to the screen. He'd disappeared.

"Where's he gone?" Peering closer, Josh could just make out an arch in the back of the gambling room. Kobayashi must have gone through it, but Josh couldn't see into the darkness beyond. "Where does that go?"

"One second," Mimasu tapped furiously on her keyboard, and the screen split in two, one half still showing the gambling room and the other showing the view from a different CCTV camera. It was a dim concrete corridor, leading to a single door. The young woman and Kobayashi walked into shot and she knocked on the door. It opened, and Josh caught the briefest glimpse of several men standing inside, before Kobayashi disappeared and the door closed firmly behind him.

Nana clicked her tongue in irritation. "We need to know what they are saying," she said. "But there's no camera in that room."

"*Deng yi huir*," Granny said, holding up her hand. She stood up, but Josh didn't catch her next words. She shuffled through the crowd and ducked under the archway right at the back of the gambling room. She reappeared on the other CCTV camera, moving along the corridor towards the back door. Then she paused right beside it, bending her head to listen.

Jessica bit her lip. "She's really exposed," she muttered. "If anyone else goes into that corridor..."

"We have to take the risk," Mimasu said. "We need to know what they're talking about in there."

Josh nodded. If he listened hard, he could just about hear men's voices coming in over Granny's microphone, speaking in muffled Japanese. He couldn't make out any of the words, though.

A movement on the image of the gambling room caught his eye, and he focused on that half of the screen again. Two men in uniform black shirts and visible earpieces were standing in the main doorway to the gambling room, looking around. One of them beckoned over a grey-haired waiter, who listened to their questions for a moment before pointing to the left of the screen...right at the empty chair where Granny had been sitting. The men strained their necks, looking around the room.

"Oh no," Josh muttered. Jessica followed his gaze and gasped.

"Granny, be careful," she whispered. "There are two men looking for you!"

Josh swallowed down a hard lump that had formed in his throat. "It's no good – she's exposed and unarmed..." He looked over at Mr. Yakamura, hoping to see a reassuring smile on the old man's face. The frown he saw instead made chills run down his spine.

"This is bad," Mr. Yakamura said. "That place is full of Yakuza. She could be massively outnumbered. We should go in."

"*You will not risk our cover,*" Granny's voice whispered in Josh's ear. "*I forbid it.*"

"Jess and I could go in," Josh volunteered, without hesitation. He looked at Jessica. She'd gone pale, but her lips were set in a thin, determined line and she nodded.

"*No, absolutely not*," Granny hissed.

"But you need backup, Mimi-san," Mr. Yamamoto said thoughtfully. "You trained them yourself – are you sure they aren't ready?" He caught Josh's eye and winked. Josh swelled with pride – Mr. Y clearly *did* believe they were ready, or he wouldn't have suggested it.

There was a heavy pause, before Granny's voice spoke again. "*They can come in to be my lookouts, no more*," she said.

Mr. Yamamoto covered his microphone and leaned close to Josh. "Do what you need to, to protect our leader. Understood?"

"*Hai*," Josh said, jumping to his feet. "Let's go!"

"And quick," Jessica said, getting to her feet. "Granny's in danger!"

Chapter Seven

Josh shoved his hands into his pockets, trying to look casual, as he and Jessica strolled towards the front door of the Omajinai.

"You can't get in past those brutes," Nana's voice said in Josh's ear. *"They'll never let a pair of children inside. There must be a back way in we can't see on our cameras. Don't go for the front door. Keep circling the building."*

"Hai," Josh murmured. They passed the door and

turned a corner into a narrow alleyway. Josh saw a row of flowering shrubs along the side of the building, but no door. Then he felt Jessica's hand gripping his elbow. She pulled him up against the wall, in a small gap among the shrubbery. She pointed upwards.

"A window!" she whispered. Josh looked up. The window ledge was a couple of metres over their heads. The glass looked dark and grimy, and the frame just wide enough for them to slip through. "Give me a leg up," Jessica said. "I'll get it open."

Josh laced his fingers together and braced his arms. Jessica stepped into his hand and he took her weight, his arm muscles straining, boosting her up until she was eye-level with the window.

"It's on a latch," she said. "I can just…" Josh heard a couple of small scraping noises, and then a click and a soft creaking. "Got it. The drop's about two metres." She leaned forward and Josh felt her weight lift off his hands. Then she slipped through the window and was gone. He heard something hitting a hard floor, and a small *oof*. "I'm in," Jessica whispered. "Can you reach, Josh?"

He looked around. The window was too high for him to grab from a standing position. He inspected the bushes, but didn't think they'd hold his weight. It was going to have to be a running jump.

"Yep," he said, backing up. "I'll be with you in a second." He walked as far back as he dared and then leaped into a sprint. His feet slammed into the ground once, twice, three times, and he sprang into the air, grabbing onto the window ledge. His momentum made him swing wildly out to one side, and his fingers almost slid off the ledge as his wrists twisted under the strain. Then he swung back again and hung there, gripping on tight.

Right. Now to pull myself up.

With a grunt of effort he managed to scramble up to the window and dive through head first. The world turned upside down as he somersaulted through and landed on his feet in the corridor below.

When the corridor had stopped spinning, he saw that they were on a landing, between the front door and a dim, narrow flight of stairs leading downwards. He could hear the faint sounds of chattering and clinking glasses from below.

"Nana, what's going on with the two men?" he whispered.

"They're still searching the main gambling room."

Josh breathed a little easier. "We're on our way."

As they descended lower and lower, the air grew thick and choking. Josh could smell cigar smoke, like the kind their English grandfather sometimes smelled of, but much more pungent and oddly spiced. The stairs were dark and claustrophobic, only just wide enough for the two of them to walk side by side. They turned a corner sharply and continued down, round and round until Josh realized he'd no idea which way they were facing.

He tried to fix the picture from the CCTV monitor in his mind. When they found the gambling room, the corridor that led to the back room would be somewhere to their right. If there was trouble, they'd need to get over there quick...

"Nana, have we found out anything useful?" Jessica asked.

"Oh indeed," came Nana's voice through their ear-buds. *"Mimasu has been enhancing Mimi-san's recordings. Minister Kobayashi sounds very upset.*

He says he has had enough. He seems to be being blackmailed – something about photographs, and some men who Kobayashi didn't know were Yakuza. Then Kobayashi says the violence is too much, he doesn't want to hurt Shini."

Josh and Jessica looked at each other, their eyebrows raised.

"Then Kobayashi's innocent...sort of?" Jessica shrugged. "But he still arranged for those things to happen to him, didn't he?"

"The question is, who's controlling him?" Josh wondered.

"*We can't tell yet*," said Nana. "*But it looks like the Yakuza are heavily involved*."

Josh swallowed hard.

They turned another corner, and found themselves standing in a large doorway decorated with kanji and Chinese lettering. Through it they could see the gambling room. It was even bigger than it had looked on CCTV. Josh could make out the first two rows of mah-jong tables, but the rest were lost in the crowd. He and Jessica pressed themselves against the wall.

"What now?" Jessica whispered.

"Get to that back corridor before the two guys figure out where Granny is. Then take them out if we need to, before they can raise the alarm," Josh said, in the most confident voice he could muster. "If we keep moving we can get through the crowd without getting caught...I hope."

"Right..." Jessica breathed.

They slipped into the hot, crowded room. One gambler gave them a slightly odd look, but Josh moved fast, ducking under someone's arm and slipping between two tables. He stopped by a bank of slot machines, peering around the room, looking for the two men in black shirts. The air was thick with the chatter of Mandarin conversation, punctuated by the clicking of mah-jong tiles and the flutter of playing cards. He thought he saw a large black-shirted shoulder moving through the crowd.

"Let's keep moving," he whispered to Jessica. They dodged around the slot machines. Josh tried to keep his head down and look out for the best way round to the back corridor.

Jessica grabbed his arm and pulled him to the

floor. They rolled under a table, just in time to see the kimono of the young waitress shuffle past.

"If the staff spot us, we're out of here," Jessica hissed. "We have to avoid them, too!"

Josh nodded. They crawled out from under the table. Josh nudged Jessica's shoulder and pointed through the forest of gamblers' legs. He could see the entrance to the corridor, only a few metres away.

"*Hurry.*" Mr. Yamamoto's voice was suddenly in his ear. "*The men are heading right for you.*"

Josh took a deep breath, grabbed Jessica's hand, and they both ran, doubled over, towards the corridor. Josh thought they would be spotted as soon as they came out of the crowd, but no outcry followed them as they dodged past the last table and made a run for it, turning the corner into the dim corridor and stopping, their backs pressed to the wall, out of sight of the gamblers.

"Did we make it?" Josh gasped.

"Think so!" Jessica edged away from the gambling room, her shoulders sagging with relief. Josh looked down the corridor and saw Granny, standing by the door with her ear to the wall. She gave him a hand signal, somewhere between *I'm fine* and *Don't come any closer*. He nodded and waved back.

"Let's hope the men didn't see us," Jessica whispered. "We can lie in wait here, and—"

"*Shimatta!*" Granny snapped. Josh looked up, his blood chilling in his veins as he watched his granny crane to listen harder, her eyes narrowing. "I know that voice!" she hissed. "It's Yoshida!"

Josh gaped. *Mr. Yoshida, the Yakuza boss? Not him again...*

Suddenly the expression on Granny's face changed and she pointed.

"Josh!" she called. "Behind you!"

Josh turned just in time to see a fist powering through the air towards him.

Chapter Eight

Josh ducked, but the fist struck a glancing blow to the top of his head. He felt a burst of pain, and his vision swam. He backed away, the corridor spinning around him.

The scene came back into focus and he saw Jessica hit their attacker square in the chest with a spinning kick. But the second man was just behind. Josh barrelled forward into him, striking with his shoulder and pushing the man back.

There was a bang, and Josh turned to see the door to the back room wide open. An elderly Japanese man with a ponytail stood there, his thin grey brows drawing together in surprise as he stared at Granny. His glance flickered over her shoulder, taking in Josh, Jessica, and their attackers.

"Why, Mimi," he said. "Always a pleasure. And your charming little—"

Granny didn't wait for him to finish. She dropped to the ground, rolled, came up behind him and planted a solid kick to the middle of his back. He stumbled forward, but turned the fall into a somersault and was on his feet again at once, twisting round to face her, his hands raised.

"Why don't you let me take my grandchildren outside," Granny said. "Then we can talk, just the two of us."

"Ah, Mimi. I have no interest in making deals, even with you. Take them!" Yoshida snapped, nodding at the men in black. One of the thugs grabbed Josh's arm and shoved him towards the wall. Josh jumped up at the last minute and planted his feet on the brickwork, pushing back with all his might. They toppled backwards and hit the ground together, rolling and tumbling along the corridor until Josh came to a rest with the man on top of him. Now Josh was on his back, and the man raised a fist to drive it into Josh's face...and then hesitated. Josh looked up. They'd rolled all the way into the main gambling room. Silence had fallen. Players, spectators and gamblers turned. A waiter gasped and dropped a tray of glasses, shattering the silence.

Suddenly, everyone seemed to be moving. Waiters and waitresses screamed and ran for the exit. The sharp-suited young Yakuza with the slicked-back hair stood and squared their shoulders. Elderly gamblers creaked and hobbled from their chairs. Tables toppled and mah-jong tiles scattered across the floor.

With a roar of annoyance, the man slammed his fist down into Josh's face – or at least, the patch of bare concrete where it had just been.

"Gaaaaaaahhh!" he screamed, clutching his hand.

Josh couldn't help but grin at the yell of pain as he ducked away under the man's arm, but he stopped smiling when he nearly caught Jessica's foot in his face. She was vaulting over him into the gambling room to escape a vicious roundhouse kick from the other man in black. They both scrambled to their feet. Josh scanned the room. Two big men in black. Three slick Yakuza – was that the glint of a flick knife he saw in one of their hands? And there was a commotion from the stairs as the two Chinese bouncers burst into the room, flexing their muscles.

Seven against two. I've seen better odds...

Granny and Yoshida spun into the room like acrobats, ducking and parrying each other's blows so smoothly they looked as if they were performing a complex dance routine.

Eight against three. Not much better... Granny hit one of the men in black in the back of the neck, and he crumpled at once. *Except one of our three is Granny! That's seven to three...*

"Fight!" Granny commanded, between spinning kicks. "We must get out of here! Head for the exit. I will follow."

The twins ran for the door. But the Chinese brutes blocked their way. One of them threw a punch at Josh, missing by millimetres. He dropped to the floor and crawled under the table, leaving the bouncer grabbing at thin air. There was a crash as the table was overturned, but he kept crawling, trying to pick his spot to come back up. He saw Jessica's feet dancing between the chairs, trying to kick them out of her way – and then he saw the shiny leather shoes and trousers of a Yakuza approaching her. Had she seen him?

Josh leaped, rising from under the tables like a shark erupting from the sea. The Yakuza paused, the gleaming silver blade raised in one hand and ready to strike towards Jessica. Josh aimed a hard chop to the man's wrist and the knife spun away.

The Yakuza let out a scream of frustration. "You little rat!"

He tried to headbutt Josh, but Josh ducked and got him on the ankle with a low kick. The Yakuza's legs buckled and he went down.

"*Nana, it's time*," Josh heard Granny say, her voice coming clear over his earphones, though she was on the other side of the room in the middle of a whirling tempest of spinning kicks.

"Hai, *I'm putting in the call*," said Nana's voice.

Josh didn't have time to ask what the call was. The other two Yakuza were upon him. He tried to back away but a fallen chair caught his legs and tripped him up. He scrambled to his feet again just in time to see Jessica thrown hard against a slot machine, making it rattle and whir.

"*Obaasan?*" Josh called. He looked around for Granny. She was still fighting Yoshida, her style efficient and calm. Between flying roundhouse kicks, low blocks and backflips, she was making her way over to the door. She threw a fierce side kick and knocked one of the bouncers into the wall, head first.

"*Use* your surroundings, Josh!" Granny shouted over the thug's yell of pain. "Agility, speed – go!"

Jessica jumped up on top of the slot machine. Josh looked back at the upset tables, understanding flooding through him.

Those aren't obstacles – they're weapons! He climbed up onto the nearest one. It wobbled under him. *Woah... Okay, I can use that too*. He threw his weight forward and used the unstable tabletop like a springboard, leaping across the room towards Jessica.

One of the bouncers grabbed for Josh's ankles as he landed on another table, but he jumped again and the brute's hands closed on thin air. Josh brought his feet down hard on his attacker's shoulders. The bouncer moaned, crumpled and hit the ground in a shower of teacups and mah-jong tiles.

"Let's get out of here," yelled Jessica. She ran along the tops of the slot machines and grabbed hold of a light fitting, swinging herself across the scattered tables like Tarzan till she got to the empty doorway.

Josh scanned the room, planning his route over the tabletops to the doorway. He jumped, dancing his way across the rickety tables that folded underneath him. He flipped onto his hands on the soft felt of a card table and pushed off again, landing on his feet on a mah-jong board near the exit.

"C'mon, Josh!" Jessica called. But Josh didn't get down. He turned and waited for just a few more seconds, until the Yakuza were closer...

Just a little closer...

Then he drew his right foot back and swung it like he was taking a penalty kick in extra time, sending the contents of the table flying into the faces of the Yakuza – teacups, a teapot and the boiling tea inside it, and a small rainstorm of hard, ceramic tiles. The young Yakuza screamed and fell back, covering their faces.

"Woo! What a move!" Jessica yelled. "Come on, let's— Urk!" Josh spun round, nearly losing his footing and falling. More guys had appeared in the doorway – four Yakuza in shiny suits and a whole bunch of hulking goons. One of them had grabbed Jessica, and had his arm around her throat; she was clawing for air, her face going red. Josh froze. The bad guys spread out through the room, cutting off all possible escape routes.

"Now," said the brute with his arm over Jessica's neck. "We don't want any—"

Suddenly, the man's arm dropped from her throat and he fell to his knees, twitching. Josh just had time to see the sparking wires from a taser gun retracting from the man's back before there was a flash, a huge bang, and thick yellow smoke flooded into the room. Within seconds, Josh could barely see a thing.

What's going on? he thought desperately.

A voice boomed into the room, in deafeningly loud Japanese. Josh couldn't fully understand what the voice said, but it was something like, "Police! Do not attempt to resist. We have all exits covered."

Josh heard the Yakuza coughing and panicking. He held his breath and clapped his sleeve over his mouth, trying to breathe slowly.

Granny seized his hand and pulled him down from the table. He saw the silhouette of Jessica standing beside her.

"Quick and quiet," Granny whispered.

They stepped over the still-twitching thug in the doorway, and climbed the stairs to street level.

"What just happened?" Josh gasped.

"Yoshida called for reinforcements," said Granny sternly, "and so did we. Now, come on, I want you two out of here."

Police officers passed them on the stairs, running down to the gambling room with gas masks and handcuffs. None of them gave the old lady and her two grandchildren a second glance until they reached the very top. A man in a particularly shiny uniform nodded to Granny as they reached the doors.

"Are you all right, *obaa-sama*?"

"*Hai*," Granny said. "Good work, officer." The policeman opened the door and bowed politely to

Granny and the twins. Josh bowed back, and then they stepped out into the neon glare of Shinjuku.

"This operation was a success," said Sachiko, pouring tea for Josh and Jessica back in Team O's headquarters, "even if not a clear victory. We learned everything we went in to find out, and a little more besides."

Josh rotated his shoulders, which were aching and stiff, and glanced at the livid bruise on Jessica's neck.

"Yoshida saw me, and he saw the children." Granny frowned into her teacup. "So he knows that we are on to him. And he and the Minister escaped. There must have been a secret exit in case of police raids."

"On a positive note," Mr. Yamamoto said, with a cheery smile and a wink at Josh, "the Omajinai will be shut down – no more filthy gambling Yakuza on that block, eh, Mimi-san?"

"Now, Yamamoto-san, it's not nice to tease your team leader," Sachiko said, just as if she was telling off a naughty little boy.

"Nana-san, any change in Kobayashi's status?"

Granny asked, with a firmly-changing-the-subject tilt of her head towards the control banks.

"No change," Nana said. "I haven't picked him up on any airport cameras, but if I were him, I would have fled the country by now. Leave Yoshida to do his own dirty work."

"I agree," said Granny. She walked up behind Nana's seat and stared at the still photographs of Yoshida, Kobayashi and Shini on the large screens. "Kobayashi was a smart choice for blackmail. The Minister for Culture won't be out of place at this kind of event and he has no criminal history. We will make sure the regular police track him down, but I think Yoshida will have cut him loose. I know how he thinks – Kobayashi was just a pawn, and one that's outlived its usefulness. Our task now is to stop one of the most dangerous criminals in the country from committing severe assault, maybe murder, to get Shini to throw the game on Saturday."

"And here's why," said Nana, tapping a few buttons. The screen went blank, then filled with lines of code on a white background. Nana highlighted part of it. "There. See the entry for Thursday, 11.43 a.m.? Just this morning, someone named Hana Nishimura placed a bet on England to win the football game. A *large* bet."

"Who's Hana Nishimura?" Jessica asked.

"Probably an alias, a fake bank account," said Granny. "Or maybe some hapless fool Yoshida has tricked into being his go-between." Granny raised her eyebrows. "When I was listening in at the gambling den, I heard Kobayashi say something about moving a large amount of...I didn't get the last part."

"Also, this is only one bookmaker," Mimasu said, slipping on a pair of reading spectacles and leaning in to scan the screen. "If I were Yoshida, I would have placed bets with everyone going. With the odds the way they are, if Shini lets England win, he will make back five hundred times what he has put in. And he has put a *lot* in." Josh stared at the figure on screen. He couldn't convert yen to pounds in his head, but he knew it was a very, *very* big number.

"The question is," Granny stroked her wrinkled chin thoughtfully, "will Shini do it?"

"No!" Josh burst out. Immediately he felt his face start to go red. Team O all stopped sipping their tea or tapping at their control panels, and looked at him. Granny turned and crooked an eyebrow. Josh looked at his sister. "Back me up, Jess, Shini would never do something like that, right?"

"I don't think so," Jessica said. Her voice was firm, but quiet. Josh frowned.

"Josh-kun," said Mr. Nakamura, "your faith in your friend is to be admired. But the truth is that we just do not know what Shini is going to do. He may not feel he has a choice. Yoshida may be applying pressure in all sorts of ways."

"We must work on the basis that he will do it," interrupted Granny. "Yoshida must be confident of success, to have placed these bets already. If Shini doesn't do it, Yoshida's funds will be hit, and badly. He must, therefore, have some information we do not."

Josh gritted his teeth. "I...suppose that makes sense," he admitted.

To his surprise, Granny put a hand on his shoulder. "And yet, we do not know what that information is. There is only one way to find out. It's time to talk to Shinichiro. And the best person to do that...is you."

Chapter Nine

"We're here to see Mickey Mouse," Granny said to the hotel receptionist.

"I believe Mouse-san is in the gym at the moment," said the receptionist, with a totally straight face.

The twins had asked Kiki for Shini's secret code name. Lots of celebrities used them, to stop any old journalist walking into hotels and pretending to know them. Kiki told them that Shini was using Mickey Mouse – Kiki often called herself Minnie.

"I can send a message to him that you are here," the receptionist went on. "Or if you like you can visit him in the gym."

"Oh, okay," said Jessica. "We'll go and talk to him there."

Granny nodded her approval. Josh could guess what she was thinking – the gym wouldn't be private, but it'd be better than the busy hotel lobby.

The gym was in the basement, and the lift doors swished open onto a gleaming corridor full of mother-of-pearl and chrome with swan motifs painted on the walls. Doors to male and female changing rooms, a sauna, a spa and a swimming pool were marked in symbols: English and kanji. Through a wall of glass panels, Josh saw a huge white space full of mirrors, high-tech gym machines and neatly stacked, colour-coded weights. It was the biggest, swankiest gym Josh had ever seen, and that included the secret government agency where Team O trained.

A tanned gym assistant with bulging muscles raised his eyebrows at the two children and the little old lady, but when they asked for Mickey Mouse he waved them through with a low bow.

They were in luck – Shini was the only person using the gym. He was running on one of the treadmills, facing a wall of mirrors, with a monitor strapped to his arm that trailed wires from his forehead all the way down to his ankle. In front of him, a flat-screen television hung from the ceiling, showing a Japanese football pundit having an argument with an English presenter. Words in both English and kanji scrolled along the bottom of the screen: *BIG GAME TOMORROW! WILL TAKESHI RECOVER IN TIME? IS GALLAGHER'S CALF MUSCLE AT RISK?*

What would they say if they knew the really urgent question – will the match be fixed? Josh wondered.

Shini looked up as Josh, Jessica and Granny walked in. He tilted his head in puzzled greeting, but he didn't slow down his run.

"Why don't you two join him?" Granny said under her breath, smiling and waving at Shini. "With one of you on either side, and me at his back, he will not try to flee."

Josh swallowed. He hadn't even thought that was a possibility. But if Shini was, for some reason, thinking of doing what Yoshida asked…he had to admit it made sense.

"All right." Jessica nodded. "You take the left treadmill, I'll take the right. We need to look as though we're here to exercise, rather than question someone, in case anyone else comes in."

"Got it," Josh replied. They stepped up onto the treadmills on either side of Shini.

"Josh," Shini said, "Jessica…Murata-sama, *ohay*. How are you? Er…what can I do for you?"

"We wanted to talk to you," Jessica said, starting her machine and walking forward on the other side of Shini.

Josh tapped the buttons on his treadmill and it whirred into life. He glanced over at Shini's LED display and increased his speed to match.

"We think…" Josh began. The treadmill was accelerating under him and he had to stop speaking while he adjusted his footing to make sure he wasn't going to go shooting off. Was Shini really going this fast? He was barely breaking a sweat! "Er, we think there's something wrong, Shini," he said. He saw Jessica tapping up the settings on her treadmill.

She wasn't going *faster*, was she? His fingers hovered over the speed setting on his own machine. *Anything you can do, sis...*

"Wrong?" Shini asked.

"Yeah, Shini, look," Jessica panted. "We know about Kobayashi."

Shini gasped and grabbed the bar across the front of the treadmill. His eyes were wide with shock, but he said nothing for a moment – just kept running. Beads of sweat were starting to creep down his cheek. He grabbed his towel and wiped them away. Josh saw him look into the mirror, glancing at Granny. She was standing right behind him, still and impassive, her hands folded in the sleeves of her traditional lavender kimono. She gave Shini a short nod. Josh saw him swallow hard.

"Kobayashi? The Culture Minister? What...do you know about him?"

"We know...he wanted you...to throw the game," Jessica panted. Out of the corner of his eye, Josh saw her surreptitiously nudge the *Speed Down* button. He felt a brief flush of victory, along with a burning sensation stinging his lungs.

"I don't know what you're..." Shini began. Then he shook his head. "No, I cannot do this." His shoulders sagged and he hit the *Off* button on his treadmill.

Josh nearly gasped with relief and slapped the same button on his machine. All three of them slowed to a walking pace, their displays flashing up *WARM DOWN: 1 MINUTE*. "I couldn't say anything," Shini muttered. "He is so powerful – a government minister! I was afraid for my family if I exposed him." He wiped his face again. "But you are Kiki's friends – I know I can trust you. How on earth did you find out?"

"Why don't..." Josh began. Even though they'd slowed down, his voice came out as a harsh whisper. A droplet of sweat fell in his eye and he blinked it away. "Why don't you tell us everything that happened?"

Shini gave a long sigh and bowed his head, as if gathering his thoughts.

"Just before we met, he found me in the changing rooms. He was the man I told you was a fan. Before he ran away, he offered me money to play badly against England, to let them win. I asked him why, but he wouldn't tell me."

"How did he seem?" Jessica asked.

"Nervous," said Shini, "like he didn't really want to be there. But he was persistent, he offered me more and more money, and when I wouldn't take it he said...he said something about my parents. That he hoped their restaurant was flourishing."

"Then, that night..." Josh prompted.

"Those thugs attacked." Shini nodded. "They were sending me a message. I got a phone call from Kobayashi, and I turned him down again. Then, of course, there was the accident at the photo shoot... I thought it might be a coincidence, really an accident..."

Josh glanced across Shini at Jessica and she nodded back at him. *You wouldn't have thought that if you'd seen the note we found in your jacket pocket*, Josh thought.

"But then Takeshi was poisoned... I presume that canapé was meant for me." A miserable frown passed over his face. "I should have gone to the police, but I was scared they would come after more of my teammates...or they would find out about Kiki..."

"It's not your fault," Josh said. "We understand. If

it helps, we don't think they know about Kiki and they're not targeting anyone else. They just want to keep you from playing at all."

Shini let out a long breath. "That is...kind of a relief..." he said, though he really didn't sound sure about it.

"Shini," said Josh. "I'm sorry, but we have to ask...you didn't tell him you would throw the game, did you?"

"What? No! I would never betray my country like that! And it wouldn't just be my country, but yours too – the whole sport would suffer."

"We know, sorry," Josh said, glancing at Granny in the mirror. She gave him a nod so small it was almost invisible.

"Kobayashi has run away," Jessica said. "But he wasn't the mastermind. The real villain is a Yakuza boss named Yoshida Noboru."

"Oh no." Shini winced. "Yakuza, really?" The three treadmills finally wound down to a standstill, and Shini turned and leaned against the control panel. "We all hear stories about organized crime, corruption and violence, even in the football business...but they're like tales of *yūrei* – ghosts and spirits." He shook his head. "I never thought I'd get caught up in something like this."

Josh and Jessica stepped off their machines, a little unsteadily.

"He's betting huge sums on England to win," Josh explained. "And he's gone ahead and placed the bets – which means that he must be pretty sure you won't play tomorrow."

"Which means – oh." Shini raised a hand to his mouth. "He's going to try to…to take me out, between now and tomorrow afternoon."

"You'll need protection from now on," said Granny. Shini looked up at her.

"And…excuse me, Murata-sama, but how do you three know all this? You are just two kids and – respectfully – a venerable old lady. I don't understand."

Josh looked at Granny, holding his breath. What could they tell him?

Granny nodded, slowly. "I think, since your life is at risk, you must know the truth. Shinichiro-san, I am the head of a team of government agents. Do not be deceived by appearances – being elders serves as our cover. Between us we have more than two hundred years of experience fighting crimes of all kinds, and Yoshida's gambling scam and his attempts on your life are both serious crimes."

Shini blinked and his mouth fell open. "But...you two," he said, looking at Josh and Jessica. "You are just...kids...right?"

"They are part of my team, Shinichiro-san," Granny said, her face utterly serious. "They will look after you."

Shini blinked under her intense glare, and swallowed. *"Hai*, Murata-sama," he said.

"Don't worry," Jessica said, patting his arm kindly. "We're a lot stronger than we look."

Although, Josh thought, mopping his forehead with his T-shirt, *apparently not a lot faster.*

"You should go to your room now," Granny advised, "and not open the door for anyone you don't trust absolutely. I will arrange for one of my team to stand guard outside. Tomorrow, we will all meet you here and ensure your safety until the match begins."

"We...we'll be going to the Gumyoji Temple in the morning," Shini said. "Down in Yokohama... We always go and receive a blessing there, before a big match."

"Then we'll be there with you," said Josh. "And we'll stick with you until you walk onto the pitch."

Josh's stomach did a backflip as Shini smiled nervously and nodded at him. A rush of pride and a twist of anxiety were fighting it out inside him, stomping all over his insides like Godzilla and Mothra taking on Tokyo.

Granny said we were part of her team, he thought. *She must really have faith in us. I swear, I'll make her proud.* But on the other hand, the responsibility was awe-inspiring: it was up to them not just to stop Yoshida, but possibly to save Shini's life. *It will be fine*, he told himself. *We can do this. We have to...*

A guard was placed on Shini's door straight away, and early the following morning the rest of Team Obaasan drove over to the hotel. When they arrived, they waited in the van, while Granny called Shini's room to check all was okay.

"He is fine," she reported, as Nana circled Josh and Jessica, carefully plugging in their earphones and attaching nearly invisible microphones to the insides of their T-shirts. "He will meet you in the lobby, and you will board the team bus with the players. People will think you're team mascots."

Mimasu pointed to one of the screens, where a map showed the team's route from the hotel to the Gumyoji Temple and then to the stadium. "We've identified that the most likely point of attack will be from the supporters gathered outside the temple. The crowd will provide a prime opportunity for Yoshida to make an attempt on Shini."

"Luckily, it will also be a perfect cover for us to move among them and keep an eye out for trouble," said Mr. Yamamoto, strapping a retractable club to one of his arms and a taser to the other.

"You'll stick with Shini," said Granny, "in case of an attempt at close quarters. Keep him in sight, and make sure he stays away from the bus windows. Good luck, and remember everything you've learned."

"*Hai, obaasan.*" Josh nodded. He had the urge to salute, but he thought that might look foolish, so he bowed his head briefly.

"We will," Jessica added. Her voice was quiet and

her face serious – that meant she was nervous, Josh thought.

The twins climbed out of the van and waited for Shini in the hotel lobby. Shini was grinning when he stepped out of the elevator, although Josh could make out subtle dark circles under his eyes. Had he had trouble sleeping? Josh's heart juddered for a second. That was one possibility he hadn't thought of – Shini could be so anxious he wouldn't play his best.

"Hi guys," Shini said. "Look what I've got." He held up two matching Team Japan sports jackets, with white stripes down the sleeves and the official Japanese Football Association logo embroidered on the back. "Now you're really part of the team. You can keep them, too, they were going spare."

"Wow!" Josh and Jessica pulled on the jackets and turned to face each other – apart from the girl/boy thing it was almost like standing in front of a mirror. They looked good. Josh put one hand in his pocket and raised the other to fix his collar, and Jessica copied him in perfect sync. Shini laughed, some of the stress in his face evaporating.

The rest of the Japanese team gathered in the

lobby. All of them seemed to be in a good mood, exchanging banter in lightning-fast Japanese and laughing. Takeshi was there too, officially recovered enough to play. Josh knew that was mostly thanks to Mr. Nakamura's in-depth knowledge of deadly poisons and their antidotes.

Yeah, as long as nobody tries to assassinate my new friend, today could still be really awesome, he thought.

As they were about to board the team bus, Mimasu was getting off, her grey hair hidden beneath a mechanic's cap. She winked as they climbed on.

"No sabotage here," she said, her quiet voice coming in loud and clear through the earphones.

For the first few minutes of the ride to the temple, Josh sat staring out of the window.

I'm riding the Team Japan bus...to a temple... wearing a Team Japan tracksuit – on the morning of a Japan–England international! He grinned across the aisle at Jessica, who was grilling Goro Sasaki about his career and his hopes for the match. She looked up from her notebook, caught Josh's eye and grinned back.

The players started up a call and response chant between the left and right sides of the bus:

"Oh ore no Nippon!"

"Kyō mo isshoni shōri mezase!"

"Nippon Nippon hai!"

"Hai! Hai! Hai!"

Something else caught Josh's attention – was it his imagination, or had someone said the name "Kobayashi"? He looked around, wondering if it was a different Kobayashi, but then realized that the tinny voice that had spoken was coming from the bus radio. It was in Japanese, but he thought he caught Kobayashi's name again and words for "government minister" and "missing".

The bus crawled through the narrow, hilly streets of Yokohama, and Josh heard distant cheering. A moment later the green, gently sloping temple roof came into view over the low buildings. People were crowding into the streets. From behind police barriers, supporters were waving red and white flags and applauding the team as they arrived for their blessing.

Josh scanned their faces, the tight knot of worry

returning to his stomach. Any one of the people in the crowd could have been sent by Yoshida to try to harm Shini – or the whole team. The group of raucous young men waving beer bottles...the middle-aged woman in a business suit... Even the two kids pressing themselves against the barrier could be plotting something nasty.

"Are you in place, *obaasan*?" he muttered.

"Hai," came Granny's voice. "*We are dispersed through the crowd. All quiet so far.*"

Josh peered at the crowd. There were a couple of elderly people there, but he couldn't make out any of Team O.

"Shini," he muttered over his shoulder, as the coach slowed. Shini was in the seat behind him and leaned forward to hear.

"*Hai?*"

"Keep away from the windows until we're in the courtyard," Josh said. Shini took a deep breath, his eyes staring into the middle distance for a second.

"...Okay." He shifted across to the second seat and piled his bag and coat up between him and the window.

At last, the bus pulled into the temple courtyard and hissed to a halt.

"Any news?" Josh said.

"*Nothing,*" Mr. Nakamura's voice replied. "*It seems Shini is safe, for now.*"

"Thanks, Mr. Nakamura," Jessica said. "Thanks, Team O!"

As the players disembarked and discarded their boots, six monks shuffled down the steps from the main hall, their black and white robes crisp and their bald heads shining in the morning sun. They bowed low to the players, who all bowed back. Josh gazed up at the temple, heaving a sigh of relief that Shini was okay. He felt his breathing calm and his heart lift, the way it always did when they visited a Japanese temple. He loved the ancient lacquered wood of the pillars and the moss-edged jade tiles on the curved roof, the gentle crunching of gravel underfoot, the faint splash of running water from a low fountain full of lilies, and the way the sun gleamed off the smiling figure of Buddha in front of the hall. The temple was so peaceful, and so old, he couldn't help feeling as if the problems of the world were fleeting and unimportant.

"The blessing is for the team only," Shini whispered. "I'll be fine while I'm inside. You can stay here with the guards. I'll yell for you if anything happens."

"Oh...all right." Josh nodded, a little reluctantly. He didn't want to break the rules of the blessing.

The players started to file into the temple with the six monks flanking them, moving silently across the gravel.

As Josh watched, one of the monks fell out of step. He stopped, shuffling his feet while he pulled on the sleeve of his robe, hitching it up on his shoulder, as if it didn't fit him properly. His exposed forearm was pale, except...

Josh narrowed his eyes. Monks did not, on the whole, have tattoos. He strained to make sense of the glimpse of red and green curling around the man's arm, and felt a shiver run over his neck and down his spine as he identified the creature in the tattoo. There were talons and fangs, and long, barbed whiskers that trailed out behind it.

"Josh!" Jessica hissed, grabbing his arm hard. "That monk's got a red dragon tattooed on his arm!"

"I see it," Josh said, through gritted teeth, as the

players started to disappear through the big wooden doors into the main hall. The tattooed man stopped fussing with his robe and walked after them.

"Josh, Josh..." Jessica was shifting her feet. "It's a Yakuza tattoo, I'm sure it is!"

"We have to stop him! Granny, can you hear me?" Josh looked at the crowd beyond the perimeter of the temple, desperate for a glimpse of Team O. But there were just too many people, and the players were starting to disappear inside the temple...

"What's going on?" Granny asked.

"We think one of the monks is a Yakuza henchman in disguise!" Jessica hissed. "They're nearly all inside – we'll have to go in with them."

"Yes," said Granny. *"Stay with Shini! We'll be with you as soon as we can."*

Still holding on to Josh's arm, Jessica set off at a super-fast casual stroll and joined the back of the team just as they reached the steps. Josh lowered his head and tried to walk like a footballer, hastily kicking off his shoes and pulling his blue jacket up high around his neck. He prayed that they'd make it inside without getting caught and thrown back out.

He even tried praying to Buddha: *Hey Buddha, I'm not actually a Buddhist, but if you could lend a hand I'd really appreciate it...*

They were climbing the steps. They were walking across the wooden porch, stepping over the threshold... they were in! Josh looked up and saw the main hall stretching out in front of him, the ancient artefacts standing on pedestals around the walls, the smoke rising from incense sticks and the large hanging tapestries of elaborate kanji and figures from history...

One of the monks was coming back. Josh grabbed Jessica and they both dived behind an enormous ornamental vase that stood beside the door. Josh watched as the monk closed the doors with a final ringing *thonk.*

The monk walked away. Josh breathed out, and felt Jessica do the same.

"Where are you, Granny?" Josh whispered, edging out from behind the vase as silently as he could.

"We're close. Just hang on."

Josh spotted the fake monk, and his heart leaped into his mouth. The man was moving fast across the polished wooden floor. He was heading straight for

Shini, like a shark going after a wounded swimmer, reaching into his robe, pulling something out...

"Oh no – what's that?" Jessica gasped.

Josh broke into a run. He pushed one of the players aside. Jessica was right behind him. He had to stop the monk, had to bring him down... He saw a glint of steel as the man raised his hand.

Josh leaped into the air feet-first, launching himself into a flying kick...

Chapter Ten

A *thud* rang out as Josh's trainer connected with the fake monk's head. Josh landed as the man fell, out cold, the knife skittering out of his hand.

A stunned silence filled the temple. The players and monks were all gaping at Josh.

Hot blood rushed to his cheeks.

You just kicked a monk in the face, he thought, as his brain caught up with his instincts.

"Josh," said Goro, the player Jessica had been

interviewing on the bus. "What is this? You just hit a monk!"

Someone grabbed Josh's arms and held them tightly. It was Takeshi.

"Wait – no, not me, it's not me you should be worried about!" Josh cried. He tried to nod towards the prone figure of the fake monk. "It's him, he had a knife! He was going for Shini!"

"He's right." Jessica found her voice. "You don't understand, he's not a monk, he's Yakuza! Look at his arm."

"Are you mad?" Goro asked, but he gazed down at the bald, robed figure lying still on the wooden floor.

"It's true," Shini said. "The Yakuza are out to get me. They want us to lose the match." A ripple of outrage and disbelief ran through the players. "They made the scaffolding fall on us – Takeshi, it was me who was supposed to be poisoned!"

Josh felt Takeshi's grip on him loosen and then fall away altogether.

"Seriously," he said, "check his arm! That's no monk."

Goro stepped closer to the unconscious man,

carefully bent down and lifted the sleeve of his robe. The players gasped at the vivid red and green dragon that roared across his skin.

Suddenly the fake monk lashed out, an uppercut punch connecting with Goro's jaw and sending him flying. He'd only been pretending to be unconscious, and he leaped smoothly to his feet, shaking his head clear and crying out *"Mokka!"*

Josh's heart pounded as he stood back, falling into his ready stance with his arms up in position to block...

Who was the man speaking to?

"Hai!" two more voices replied. The players turned. Out of the five remaining monks, Josh saw two more men step forward, reaching into their robes. Each of the fake monks pulled out a pair of shiny wooden sticks, polished and dark with handles jutting out about a fifth of the way down their length.

"Tonfa," he heard Jessica mutter. "Oh, *great*."

There was a *click*, and Josh spun round again to see that the first monk had scrambled to the door and locked it.

"No!" he gritted his teeth. "Granny, they've just locked us in!"

He heard Mr. Yamamoto's voice cursing in his earphone.

"Don't worry," Granny's voice said. *"We'll find another way in."*

The real monks backed away, as the fake monks let out a yell and charged towards the players, their tonfa held up, ready to swing.

"It's up to you two for the moment," Granny said. *"I know you can handle this!"*

"Get back!" Josh yelled to the players. "Those things'll break your skulls, get back!" He had to do something to stop them. He raced towards the charging monks, past Jessica, who was pushing the players back to the corner of the room while looking over her shoulder, ready to repel a blow if she had to. A Yakuza-monk brandished his tonfa as they drew closer, twirling one of the batons through the air with a sound like ripping cloth.

Josh stopped, waited – he had to time it right, just half a second longer, until he could see the whites of their eyes and the vivid greens, reds and blues of their tattoos...

He dropped to the floor in a spinning move, his

outstretched leg sweeping around. He caught the fake monks hard on the sides of their ankles. They toppled and landed in a groaning heap in the centre of the room.

But as Josh stood up, they were getting to their feet too. Jessica sprinted up to his side, and they faced the three Yakuza-monks in a defensive stance with their feet apart and their hands raised, perfectly balanced for any attack.

"We won't let you harm any of the players," Josh said.

The monks didn't answer. A hard wood tonfa arced through the air towards Josh's head and he leaped back, almost stumbling, as one of the deadly weapons passed a few centimetres from his chin. Jessica lunged forward with a series of fast-swinging kicks, high then low, but her target raised his arms, with the tonfa shielding him, and deflected her blows as fast as she could strike.

The other two monks advanced on Josh and he scanned the room, trying to think fast and avoid their vicious blows. He ducked under an arm and landed a satisfying, heavy punch to the man's stomach, but he paid the price as a tonfa smacked down on his back. It was a weak blow, but it burned with the intensity of a hundred bee stings, and Josh had to drop and roll to avoid the next strike splintering his jaw.

...*Splintering*. That gave him an idea.

"Aim for the tonfa!" he yelled.

"I – can – hardly – avoid – them!" Jessica cried back, punctuating her words with sweeping kicks that mostly connected with nothing but thin air.

"No, really go for them." Josh ducked again to avoid one of the swinging sticks. "Like the boards we used to break in class, back in London, remember?"

"*Oh*..." Jessica danced back a few steps, a faint smile of understanding lighting her eyes.

Josh sprinted forward, right at his attackers, and threw himself into a somersault that took him right between them and left him standing behind their backs. He landed a punch on one of the monks' necks, making him stagger and let out a stream of Japanese that was very un-monklike indeed.

Beyond, Josh saw Jessica kick out at the monk she was fighting, making him raise his arm once again to deflect her with one of his tonfa. But she pulled back and before he could move she leaped, and with a yell of *"Haiiiiya!"* drove the side of her foot into the wooden stick.

"Yaaaow!" The monk cried out in pain and dropped the tonfa. It fell to the floor and lay there, one end of it splintered and now close to useless. The monk staggered back, clutching his arm, and Jessica pressed her advantage, bringing her other foot up and then down in a smashing kick onto the man's other arm, breaking the second tonfa clean in two and reducing the monk to a whimpering heap on the floor.

"Aieee!" One of the men attacking Josh twirled his tonfa in his hands and drove the ends forward in a cruel, stabbing motion.

In one smooth movement Josh ducked his head and lunged forward. The tonfa brushed through his hair, much too close for comfort, and slid into the collar of his Team Japan jacket. He unzipped it, twisted his body free, and at the same time caught the man's hands and his tonfa up together in a knot of blue fabric.

"What...?" The monk stared at him in surprise before Josh tore the bundled tonfa out of his hands and threw them towards the Japanese team. Shini caught them effortlessly, and the players cheered.

One to go, Josh thought, kicking out and catching the still-surprised monk a heavy blow to the ribcage.

"You…little…" the man gasped, and then collapsed in a heap at Josh's feet.

The last armed man was running towards the players now, letting out a scream of rage and twirling his tonfa so fast they were a solid circular blur around his hands.

"Jess!" Josh cried. "Get him!" Jessica tried to throw herself into the path of the monk as he passed, but he dodged round her. The world turned to treacle as Josh saw the monk getting closer and closer to Shini. He looked around for something, anything…and spotted the incense sticks on the low altar. They were set into grooves in heavy stone blocks, each the size of a brick. He grabbed one of the blocks and threw it, as hard as he could, hoping with his entire being that it would fly true.

The stone hit the spinning tonfa, shattering them both! The monk skidded to a halt, throwing his hands up over his face to protect himself from a shower of splinters.

"We've found a way in," Mr. Yamamoto's voice said in Josh's ears. *"Hold on just a little longer, kids!"*

Jessica raised her hands with a whoop of victory, and the football players all let out a rousing cheer... but it wasn't over. Josh saw one of the disarmed monks getting to his feet, seizing a golden statue of the Buddha from its pedestal and holding it over his head.

One of the real monks started forward, his eyes blazing. "A thousand years of history you hold in your hands," he said. "You already defame our temple – you wouldn't dare!"

Yes, they would dare, Josh thought, quickly translating in his head what the monk had just said. *But they won't get away with it!*

The fake monk grinned, showing a mouthful of gold teeth, and threw the statue to the ground.

Josh launched himself forward into a skid, sliding along the polished floor like a baseball player heading for a home run, his hands outstretched. The Buddha landed in his lap and he set it down carefully.

He looked up in time to see two of the monks charging the footballers again, their bare hands out and ready to do damage even without their weapons.

There was a loud *BANG*. An inner door had been thrown open and six lithe figures in full black ninja outfits rushed in. One of them ran up to the stunned footballers and gestured towards the door.

"Come on, all of you, out this way," said the ninja. That was Sachiko!

Josh and Jessica whooped and gave each other a high five as Team Obaasan ran, jumped and flipped across the temple towards the Yakuza fighters.

It was the first time Josh had ever seen Team O fighting all together, and it took his breath away. He tried to make out the individual members among the spinning, kicking, backflipping group, but the kicks and punches flew so fast he could barely follow them. One ninja struck a Yakuza-monk with a chopping motion on the side of his neck and another grabbed his shoulders and yanked him into a wrestling throw. Another Yakuza-monk was trying to grab at a ninja's hood, but a blurred spinning kick sent him crashing to the floor, clutching his wrist and bleeding from the chin. The final Yakuza fighter was caught between two punches, one to either side of his stomach, and crumpled like paper.

One of the ninjas, tall and lithe with stern, wrinkled eyes behind the slit of her ninja hood, walked up to Josh, Jessica and Shini. "You're safe now," she said to Shini. "Yoshida's final attempt has failed. The Yakuza will not win this day."

"Thank you...obaasan," Shini said, bowing deeply. The ninja gave a "humph" of approval, bowed back, and then raised a finger to her lips. "Of course," Shini said quickly, "not a word." Josh and Jessica grinned at each other.

"Come on," Josh said. "Let's get you to that match!"

Chapter Eleven

The whistle blew for half-time, and a huge, rolling wave of cheers circled Yokohama Stadium, echoing back and forth between the stands. Josh and Jessica leaped out of their seats and leaned over the balcony of the VIP box, cheering along with the Japanese supporters.

"One-nil! One-nil!" Jessica sang. Kiki jumped up and joined her. "Oooonne…niiiiiiil!" Josh had never heard anyone harmonize a football chant before, but it sounded awesome. Granny clapped politely beside them.

The eight seats in the VIP box were all upholstered in red velvet with little trays for drinks and snacks. Only one was empty. The other seats were occupied by two men and a woman, smartly dressed in stiff grey suits – probably executives on a corporate trip – who regularly shot them disapproving glances.

They can disapprove all they like, Josh thought. *We've earned our seats a hundred times over!*

Josh felt a rush of pride as he gazed down at the half-time cheerleaders, their red and white striped skirts swishing as they tumbled and backflipped across the pitch in formation. It was down to him and his twin sister that the teams were playing at all. He just hoped Shini kept playing well, so that Yoshida didn't win his bet.

It's a bit weird, cheering for Japan to beat England, Josh thought. *But to defeat Yoshida, I can deal with it!*

As the players ran back on for the second half, singing from the English fans filtered down from the stands and mingled with the rhythmic, syncopated drumming of the Japanese supporters. The TV cameras swooped back and forth on their cranes. The scoreboard flashed a bewilderingly fast stream of kanji which resolved themselves into the words *GO JAPAN GO*.

Kick off! Japan had possession at once, but the ball was stolen with a clever bit of misdirection by Mark Gallagher, and he zipped towards the Japanese goal. Then Goro got in the way of Gallagher's pass and booted it back towards the England end...

Granny Murata's mobile phone rang, and she fished it out of the little beaded purse that hung from the belt of her kimono. "Ah, it is Nana-san," she said, flipping open the phone. "Hello?"

Josh held his breath, his heart pounding and his attention torn from the pitch for a moment. Had something gone wrong? Was there another threat to Shini...?

Granny nodded, her eyes narrowing. "That is good news," she said. "Thank you, Nana-san. Excellent work." Josh's heart slowed to a steady thud as she hung up and turned to him with a satisfied smile. She motioned for him and Jessica to lean close to her.

"Minister Kobayashi has been apprehended," she said, keeping her voice low so the executives couldn't hear over the roar of the crowd. "Nana's surveillance operation caught him as he attempted to check in at Tokyo airport."

"That's fantastic!" Josh beamed.

"Kobayashi is willing to testify that Yoshida was behind it all. It's not enough to take Yoshida down yet, but the Minister will be a valuable asset for the police as long as Yoshida doesn't find out we have him."

"Like the ace up our sleeve!" Jessica said.

"Or the East Wind tile hidden in our kimono," Josh joked, remembering Granny's talent for mah-jong.

"Indeed," said Granny, her face deadpan.

The crowd made an "*Oooooooohhh!*" noise, and Josh's attention flicked back to the pitch again. One of the Japanese players was on the ground in the England penalty box, with an England player standing over him, gesticulating wildly. The referee held up a card – penalty to Japan!

Josh watched, holding his breath as Takeshi took the kick...and sent it speeding past the goal. A groan went up from the Japanese supporters.

Josh heard a chuckle from behind them. "*Konnichiwa*, Mimi," said an elderly man's voice. "I shan't pretend I'm surprised to find you here."

Josh, Jessica and Kiki all spun around to find Yoshida Noboru standing in the box. He bowed low to Granny Murata then stroked back his long silver ponytail and met Josh's eyes.

"And hello to you, precious grandchildren," he said, grinning like a shark. Josh fought the urge to shudder. "Mikiko-san, how nice to see you again."

"*Nice?*" Kiki gasped. "You...you horrible old man! You had me kidna—"

"Now," Yoshida said, his voice low but a nasty smile still plastered on his face. "Let's not dig up ancient history, for which there is no proof, eh?"

"Ancient history?" Jessica growled. "That was three weeks ago!"

Yoshida gave a little shrug and turned to the three executives. To Josh's dismay, they each rose politely to shake his hand, exchanging a few words of greeting as if they had all met before. Were they corrupt business leaders, in Yoshida's pocket?

Josh balled his hands into fists. He wanted to take Yoshida down right now – Jess could distract the man while Josh got in just one good punch to the back of Yoshida's neck...

He glanced at Granny. She met his eyes, briefly, and gave the tiniest shake of her head.

"I am surprised you did not come for the first half of the match, Noboru," she said in a pleasant, even tone of voice. "Or perhaps you could not bear the uncertainty of the outcome? You know how unpredictable these games can be." She indicated the scoreboard.

Josh saw Yoshida's eyes narrow and the twitch of a muscle in his cheek. His monks had failed in their mission and now the game couldn't be thrown. *He's furious, but he can't show it*, Josh thought. Yoshida's glance flickered over the pitch to Shini, safe in the Japanese goal. A cloud passed across his face for just an instant, before he recovered himself.

"I'm sure the end result will be pleasing," he muttered.

Granny snorted. "So like you, to care only about the bottom line."

Yoshida nodded. "So like *you*, Mimi, to care about fair play."

Kiki spoke up. "Shini's the greatest, and we're going to win!"

"We will see," said Yoshida, and turned to watch the game, smiling.

He looks suspiciously confident, Josh thought. Did he have some other plan up his sleeve?

Granny beckoned Josh closer.

"Do not worry," she whispered. "As well as Noboru knows me, I know him. That smile is hiding his desperation – he has no plan but to hope that the game goes his way. Watch his face when the Japanese players do well, and you will see."

Back on the pitch, the match was hotting up. A glance at the giant electronic scoreboard told Josh that there was only half an hour to go.

The England supporters roared and stamped in time as Clarkey got the ball at his feet and passed it up to Neil Ash, who sprinted for the Japan goal – but lost control at the last second, a Japan defender tackling the ball away.

Josh glanced at Yoshida. Sure enough, the

dangerous smirk didn't leave his lips, but his eyes were narrowed and angry.

Takeshi got the ball and booted it hard at the England goal. It spun as it shot through the air, and Josh gasped. But it wasn't quite on target, and the England goalie Dave "the Giant" Levy caught it easily. The twins sank back in their seats, as the England crowd yelled their approval.

"This is just too weird," Jessica muttered. "Bad enough cheering against our home team, but rooting for Japan while the Yakuza boss in the next seat supports England? That's just not right!"

Josh nodded, and laughed to hide his nerves.

The minutes and seconds ticked away in a blur of sprinting, passing, shooting and tackling. Fifteen minutes passed, then twenty, twenty-five, twenty-seven... Kiki stood again, dancing from foot to foot in anxiety. Twenty-eight, twenty-nine...

"Yes! Full time!" Jessica jumped up, pumping her fist in the air. "One-nil!"

I can't celebrate yet, Josh thought. *There's still extra time – I won't jinx it!*

Still, Yoshida looked pretty sick.

One of the referees held up a digital display that read *THREE MINUTES EXTRA TIME*. Japan just had to hold on to their lead for three more minutes...

Clarkey leaped forward with the ball and Josh's breath caught in his throat. The England players were stepping up, playing better than they had all match! The Japan team hardly got a touch in as the ball passed smoothly from Clarkey to Gallagher, back to Clarkey, then to Brown, Ash, Elton...

Jamie Elton skidded to a halt in front of the goal, avoiding a tackle from Goro, and kicked the ball up, on target, towards the corner of the goal... Shini leaped, but Josh already knew it was too far away for him. He wasn't going to catch it. Sure enough, the ball slipped between the tips of his fingers and the goalpost and hit the back of the net.

Yoshida leaped to his feet and let out an excited yell as Jamie Elton threw himself into a quadruple backflip in celebration, before the rest of his team piled onto him, patting his back and rubbing his head.

Josh groaned, as the England supporters cheered and chanted. That was a *fantastic* goal. Any other day he'd have been replaying it over and over, but this time, he felt cold shock crawling over his skin.

Shini kicked the ball as hard as he could, but it was no good.

Three, two, one...

The whistle blew.

"It's a draw!" Jessica gasped.

Kiki frowned. "Does that mean Yoshida gets his money – or not?"

"It's not over," Josh said. "They're going to penalties."

He looked over at Yoshida, who seemed stressed. A few strands of long silver hair had fallen out of his neat ponytail. Josh realized he'd started chewing his lip. Shini was the greatest goalie in the world, even better than the Giant – that had to mean that Japan would win a penalty shootout, right? *Right?*

"Each team will take turns to try to score a goal," Jessica was explaining to Kiki. "They get five goes each. They keep taking the penalties until there's a clear winner."

"I see..." Kiki frowned. "So it's really up to Shini, now."

Shini and the Giant joined the referee for the coin toss, and Shini raised his hand, waving up at the crowd, to show that Japan had won and they'd go first.

The Giant took his place in the goal, and Jun Fujita squared up to the ball on the penalty mark. The entire stadium seemed to hold its breath… Fujita took a run up, the ball went flying…and the Giant leaped the wrong way. The ball thudded into the back of the net.

1-0! proclaimed the scoreboard.

The teams swapped places. Shini waved up at the crowd again – and this time, he seemed to be waving right at Josh and the others. Kiki waved back, her other hand pressed tight across her heart. Neil Ash took the first England kick, but Shini leaped higher and faster than Josh had ever seen, and he saved the goal.

"It looks like your little gamble isn't going to pay off, Yoshida!" Kiki said.

"We will see," Yoshida snarled.

The next Japanese strike found its way into the goal. Then Jamie Elton stepped up to the ball, barely pausing before sending it soaring through the air. It hit Shini's arm, but spun and bounced chaotically between the grass and the goalposts, and finally rolling over the line before Shini could turn and grab it.

2-1!

Kiki looked like she might burst into tears.

"We're still one up," Jessica said.

Daisuke Takeda stepped up...and missed. The ball went wide, flying into the stands. Josh clamped his hands tight onto the railing as Frankie Reed took the ball, squared up to Shini, drew his foot back... and missed!

It was Takeshi's turn. Jessica screamed her encouragement. Josh couldn't – his throat and his chest felt so tight he was afraid if he opened his mouth his lungs would try to climb out. But when Takeshi's kick propelled the ball smoothly between the Giant's legs and into the goal, Josh cheered along with the others.

"It's 3-1," Jessica said, breathlessly. "England could still equalize...but they've got to get this next one. If Shini saves it, we've won."

"Come on, Shinichiro-san!" Granny called out, rising from her seat for the first time in the whole match. "For Japan! For justice!"

Josh grinned. "You can do it, Shini!" he yelled.

Daniel Akimbe lined up to take the penalty for England. He ran up and kicked, and the ball flew to Shini's right. Josh gasped as Shini twitched to his left, then changed direction at the last second, pushing off from the ground and throwing himself in front of the ball. It hit him in the chest and he clamped his arms around it as he fell.

Save!

Kiki and Jessica hugged each other and jumped up and down, their ear-piercing shrieks of joy making Granny flinch, despite her smile. The giant scoreboard flashed, red circles spiralling all over it for a second, and then the words, in kanji and English:

1-1 DRAW! JAPAN WIN 3-1 ON PENALTIES!

Kiki pulled Josh into a hug and ran out of the VIP box. *Where's she going?* Josh wondered.

Yoshida's face looked like thunder. He glared at the twins and then at Granny.

"Congratulations," he said, through gritted teeth.

"Well played, Mimi. But don't celebrate too soon. Your little troupe hasn't seen the last of me."

"I don't doubt it, Noboru," Granny said calmly.

"Get him, Granny!" Jessica said.

Yoshida laughed. "Attack me? With so many witnesses? I don't think so." He turned and stalked out of the box, slamming the door behind him.

"Granny, why *don't* we just take him down?" Josh asked.

Granny shook her head. "No. That is not how we will defeat him, children – but believe me, we will defeat him." She smiled at Josh. "After all, I have you two on my team."

Josh and Jessica beamed at each other.

There was a chorus of whistling and catcalls from the stands. Josh looked down to see that Kiki had burst out of the tunnel. She ran across the pitch to Shini and threw herself into his arms. Every photographer in the stadium turned their camera on them, but the couple didn't care. Josh and Jessica whooped and yelled, and even Granny laughed as she politely applauded.

Josh looked up at Jessica, and they exchanged

twin grins. Another week, another mystery solved, another life saved. Yoshida could swear revenge all he liked – but right now, Josh felt invincible. Whatever the next mission might be, he was ready for it.

Bring it on!

Don't miss more
high-kicking ninja action
from Josh and Jess in...

ISBN 9781409515104

ISBN 9781409522041

Coming soon